I0669075

Ice Whine and Irish Cheddar

Judy Volhart

Published by Open Books

ISBN-10: 0997806281

ISBN-13: 978-0997806281

PROLOGUE

Turning to face Matt, I leaned forward for a long kiss. When we came up for air, he angled his head to speak into my ear. "You have an entire drawer full of thongs, and I want to see each and every one of them!"

My cheeks blazed at the reminder. With a Mona Lisa smile, I whispered a suggestion: "My parents may be at my house, but that doesn't mean we can't go to your place for a little fashion show," I said with what was supposed to be a silky voice but came out more like a horny croak.

If he took notice, he didn't let on. Instead, his answer was a surprised smile coupled with a sharp intake of breath. Then, before either of us had time to come to our senses, he grabbed my hand and started to drag me in the direction of the door. Just as we got there, it burst open. There stood Nora with a pig in tow.

"We're moving in," she announced. "Where can I put my pig?"

1

CHAPTER ONE

No! This couldn't be happening, I screamed in my head. What did I have to do to get a break? It had been more than two years since I had been with someone intimately, and I wasn't even sure my parts still worked. Reluctantly, we joined Nora outside and watched in dismay as she paced frantically while the pig stood by unconcerned. I was puzzled as to how she had gotten the pig here as she normally drove a Smart car. She stopped pacing and stood with her hands on her hips.

"If I have to stay there one more minute, I'm going to kill him. All I've heard these days is whining and complaining about how I racked up the credit cards over Christmastime and how from now on he's going to be in charge of the money and the presents and this and that." Bits of spittle flew about, and I dodged left to avoid being in the line of fire.

"So where can I put Chicha?" she asked again.

"Nora, you know the pig can't come inside, it's a bistro. I'm pretty sure it would be a health code violation." I neglected to mention that, with my parents visiting, there was also a very strong possibility that the pig would end up

3

in the slow cooker.

"Maybe I can set her up inside the garage?"

I looked sadly at the detached garage and the little pathway that led to the house/bistro. That would mean I'd have to park outside, in the harsh Ottawa winter. The thought elicited a deep, selfish sigh, and I immediately felt guilty. I wasn't usually so self-centered; it was just that I really despised the cold and snow. Ottawa winters could be brutal, and this winter was proving to be the worst in one hundred and fifty years. I looked back at them and my heart wrenched at the sight of their sad eyes looking at me in expectation. It seemed as though a tiny tear had formed in Chicha's left eye. Was that even possible?

"Alright... Let me get my car out of there and we'll set something up for Chicha. I'll get you a set of keys while I'm at it. My parents are here though, so the spare room is occupied. You're welcome to sleep on the couch, but maybe you'd prefer to bunk at Nicole's tonight?" I suggested rather hopefully. While I loved Nora dearly, having my parents there was already too much for my fragile nerves. Then, unable to contain my curiosity any longer, I asked, "How did you manage to get the pig here?"

"I took the man's van," she replied, a crazy blaze returning to her eyes. I still wondered how she got it in and out of the vehicle but before I could ask she stomped back into the Bistro and plunked herself down at the bar, leaving me with Chicha. We blinked at each other but the pig didn't seem overly concerned. She knew she had a home for the night, and the tear in her eye was gone now.

Heaving another deep sigh, I apologized to Matt. "I guess we'll have to reschedule our, uh, plans. Maybe Sunday night?" I suggested hopefully. It was now Friday. Surely within a couple of days I'd convince Nora to go home, and my parents would also be gone by then.

He curved his sensuous lips into a playful pout then gave me a long, full-length hug, setting my nerve endings back on fire. "It's okay. With your concussion, you have to

4

take it easy anyway, and while I hate to admit it, it's probably a good thing we were interrupted. I'm not certain I would have been sufficiently gentle." He purred into my ear, sending goosebumps throughout my body. "I'll swing by on Sunday and remember, you can't work for a few days," he reminded me before heading off to his car.

Ah yes, I had almost forgotten that my injuries were preventing me from working at my own bistro or doing anything strenuous. If I had to be honest, I had every intention of ignoring the doctors' orders even though they were at the forefront of my mind.

My name is Amalia Kis. I'm five feet, nine inches of normalness, other than my quirky personality. Long caramel-colored hair that I try to keep straight, reaches the middle of my back and I have brown eyes and high European cheekbones. Matt and I had started dating a few weeks ago, after Joey, a friend of his, had been murdered and his body had been found, by none other than me, in my newly-purchased bistro. Matt became my self-declared body guard, wanting to help find justice for his murdered friend and to get to know me better. He never charged me a dime, but then again, he did own the security guard and private investigation company. I'm pretty sure he had some form of sexual repayment plan in mind, anyway.

After a couple of break-ins, two concussions, another murder and a near-death experience, I was ready to take the next step with Matt, having been single for too long and with him being far too sexy for me to even try to resist.

Unfortunately, with my parents visiting, and soon to be moving just a couple of miles away from me, and now with Nora hell bent on moving in, being alone with Matt was proving to be a challenge. Of course, I wasn't one to back down from a good challenge. If anything, it just strengthened my determination.

After moving my car out of the garage, I joined Chicha, who was still standing in the same spot as earlier but now had a group of people crooning over her. I led her into the garage (which meant I had to push and pull and beg her to follow me, losing my footing in the slippery snow in the process and landing on my rear end at one point), and then gave her head a quick pat and promised to return with food and blankets.

Nora was still at the bar, deep in conversation with Nicole. I hid a smirk as I noted the name of the bottle of wine she was drinking: Old Fart. No doubt she had chosen it in honor of her current opinion about The Man who was driving her crazy. I poured myself just one tiny mouthful of the blend of Grenache and Syrah grapes and savored the slightly spicy but juicy flavor wrapping itself around my tongue. I then poured another mouthful, nudging aside my common sense that was trying to remind me about my concussion.

Nicole's' eyes were still rimmed with red, but she had concealed it fairly well. She was a chronic online dater, searching for Mr. Right while her biological clock was no doubt ticking. Like me, she was thirty years old and single. We had been best friends since the age of twelve but were opposites in many ways.

She was five feet, three inches tall, a tiny little blonde thing, outgoing, loud, sometimes flashy, and hoped to one day have kids. I, on the other, was fairly certain I didn't want any. I didn't think I'd have enough energy for one, since my thyroid condition made life in general challenging enough. Running my bistro took every ounce of my strength. Plus, they were kind of smelly and I had an overly sensitive gag reflex.

She was a graceful dance instructor and a talented singer; I was dark-haired, tall and goofy and drank wine for a living, or rather served wine. And let's not forget the cheese!

Just two days earlier, Nicole had found out that a man whom she had met online and had gone out with only once, but who she suspected was following her, had been arrested for the abduction and murder of an eleven-year-old girl who was also a petite blonde like herself. Of course it had jarred her, and I hoped it would be the end of her online dating for a while.

Unfortunately, she hadn't faired any better when, by chance, she met a police officer who turned out to be engaged. That had landed him a nice slap on his cheek as way of adieu and a bonus little bitch-slapping session with his fiancé, but what was most unfortunate was that Nicole had actually started to fall for him.

As we sat in silence, the fourth member of our little group joined us. She had a quizzical look on her face. "Whatchya all so glum about?" Chloé asked, with a wide grin on her face. She, too, was small, with curly black hair and an olive complexion. She was the youngest in the bunch, only twenty, however she was an old soul trapped inside a young body. She'd not had a good childhood but was always hopeful and full of boundless energy.

Nora was the first to answer: "I left the man. He's driving me to drink!"

Chloé looked at me questioningly, not sure how to respond since Nora had always been fond of the drink. Coming to the rescue, I leaped up, then quickly sat down as black dots floated across my vision from the concussion. I could feel them all watching me and I quickly held up my hand. "I'm fine; I just got up too fast."

"We have to get Chicha some blankets and some food," I told Nora as I waited for the spots to fade. "She's all set up in my garage, but I'm sure she's nervous out there all alone."

Chloe squealed with delight. "Chicha's here? I'll get her some food and bring it out." And with that she dashed off in her ridiculously high heels to the kitchen in search of vegetables.

"Nora, were you able to ask Nicole if you could stay a night or two while I try to get my parents to go back to Montreal?" I asked.

7

Nicole was quick to respond: "By all means, Nora. I could use the company to keep my mind off things." With the arrangement settled, I went upstairs to my living quarters in search of old blankets.

It still felt strange at times, owning a house and bistro all in one. After a failed six-year relationship with pretty boy Hans, I'd sold a condo that I owned in downtown Ottawa and bought an old, renovated house that once had housed a failed restaurant. Since this house was at the very edge of Ottawa in an area known as the Village of Robin, my meager dollars stretched further. It had suited my needs and my almost non-existent budget perfectly.

The downstairs portion was my bistro, my life-dream, my joy, The Whine and Cheese, where I served wines with quirky names, cheeses and salamis, and a daily hot dish that was easy to make. My staff, for now, consisted of my friends who helped me out part-time, and since I was the bistro's cook, I kept things fairly simple and as fuss-free as possible. This wasn't haute cuisine, just a comfy and trendy place to hang out and have a few drinks, a few laughs and a nibble. I could never do anything overly fancy as it would require far too much energy that I knew I could not sustain, and quite simply, I just wasn't a fancy person.

The upstairs portion consisted of my living quarters; two bedrooms, one bathroom, large kitchen with a pantry and a large dining/living area. It was perfect for me and my cat Hummer, but not so perfect when my parents decided to visit.

Their most recent visit had proved to be catastrophic. They had decided to move to Ottawa, and as luck would have it (not good luck, I might add), they found a home only two minutes away from my own. I vowed never again to enlist the services of the realtor that I had arranged to help them, as I had very specifically told her to find something as far away from me as possible. I was not sure if my sanity could endure having 'The Aliens' living so close by, especially after having lived over two hours away

8

from them for the past decade.

I had been affectionately referring to them as The Aliens since my teenage years, but never to their faces, of course. I would never have deliberately hurt their feelings. They're Hungarian, and extremely stuck in their ways. Both speak only broken English. They've never acted Canadian, and everything was, and still is, always about the "old country" with them. I know they love me, and I love them dearly too, but I just love them more when they live a good two or more hours away. After having grown up with a maddeningly strict upbringing, I still struggled to exert my independence whenever they were around. This would definitely be a major setback for me.

They were still awake and watching TV in the living room as I searched the linen closet. My cat, Hummer, prowled around my feet, giving me a sniff. To my horror, my parents had somehow managed to find an old (and by old, I mean ancient) re-run of the Lawrence Welk show, a man who had died over twenty years ago. They seldom watched anything more modern unless it was the news, but even then, they claimed most of what was in the news was lies or half-truths.

When they asked me what I was up to, I reluctantly explained that I needed some old sheets or blankets for my friend's pig that was staying in my garage.

"A pig?" my dad asked. "Why you have pig? Is for eating? You vant I get the knife?"

"Oh, no! This is a friend's pet. Don't even think of cooking that pig!" Images of my childhood came flooding back of my parents bringing home a freshly butchered pig cut down the middle and then the sight of them cutting the rest into the desired pieces and putting it in the freezer. Or the pig on the outdoor spit, roasting over flames. Okay, maybe that last part wasn't such a bad memory. My mouth watered involuntarily. Vegetarian I am not.

"Pet? That's stupid. Who has pig for pet?"

"I'll explain later; I've got to go," I said as I grabbed

what I needed and made a speedy retreat, tripping over the cat in my haste and earning a surprised hiss. On top of that, my budding pseudo-aneurism was beginning to rear its ugly head, the vein above my left eye throbbing rhythmically. My evening certainly had taken a turn for the worse.

I joined Nora in the garage, giving her the old sheets and an old blanket. While I was away, she had also pulled a bale of hay out of the back of the van and spread it out for Chicha, who had now settled down and looked happy as...well, a stereotypical pig in shit. I made a mental note not to forget to have the garage hosed down before I parked my car in there again. It's not that I am a germaphobe, because I'm not. Not really. Okay, maybe a little.

With some last minute instructions on what to feed the pig the next day, she went back to the bar to have more wine while waiting for Nicole to end her shift. The bistro would still be open another two hours, but my head was pounding and all I could think of was my bed. I told Nicole to lock up without me and that I'd tidy up the next morning so she didn't have to stick around for that.

It was eight o'clock a.m. when I opened my eyes. A brief moment of panic raced through my body when I discovered my right leg was paralyzed. As I became more alert, I was relieved to find that it was only temporary, as it was caused by the weight of my cat sleeping on it. I was a big softie when it came to Hummer, the current and only love of my life. I let him sleep on me a while longer, until I could no longer ignore the persistent call of my bladder.

"Sorry, bud, time to wake up," I said as I moved gently to ease him off of me. He growled softly, showing his displeasure. I made him a nest with the comforters. "Look how cozy; c'mon, lie back down. There you go. Who's my good boy?" We bumped our noses together and I kissed his fuzzy head. I'd had him from the time that he was four weeks old and our bond was very strong.

"Morning," I mumbled grumpily to my parents, who were already up and with whom I did not have a strong bond, nor did I bump noses with. Moments later I joined them for coffee and sprang into action with project "send parents home".

I pasted on a determined smile. "So, as you can see, I'm feeling much better now, and the murderer is caught. My friend Nora needs a place to stay for a little while, so will you be returning to Montreal in order to start packing for your move here?" My parents lived about twenty minutes outside Montreal, and the move was set for two weeks from now.

"Ya, ve going after brekfest," my dad replied in English. It always flustered me when my parents spoke English, since they would normally only speak to me and my brother, Stephen, in Hungarian.

"You said Stephen is going to rent a moving van for you, right? When you get here, we'll all help you unpack, and don't worry about food. As we arranged, I'll be getting the key for you from the real estate agent the day before and I'll make sure your fridge is full and everything is clean so you'll have nothing to worry about." They were getting up in years and being the good daughter that I was, I wanted to make the move a bit easier for them. I might not be happy about the move, but there was nothing I could do to prevent it now.

My mom leapt up and dashed into the spare room. She was soon back, rummaging around inside her purse. "Here, you take," she said, shoving a handful of hundred dollar bills at me.

"No! I want to be able to help, it's a present from me to you, and I don't want your money. Put it away." My mother kept insisting and finally reached over and shoved it down the back of my PJ pants.

"Fine," I grumbled. I'd learned long ago that there was no winning against them. I can say and have said many negative things about them, but there's no disputing the fact that they are the most generous people I know.

They helped me tidy up after breakfast and in less than half an hour they were on the road. I could feel my mood lifting. I changed the bedding in the spare room and threw a load into the washing machine then straightened things out to my liking. My parents had moved a thing or two around, and while I tolerated it during their visit, it nagged at me now.

Remembering Chicha, I went out to feed the pig but stopped halfway down the path to the garage. The side door was slightly open and my heart sank as I picked up the pace.

I turned on the light and looked about. No Chicha. Nora was going to kill me! I was just turning to leave when a spot of black caught my eye. Sighing with relief, I walked to the back corner of the garage that had a tarp over a bunch of lawn furniture that I had stored back there. "I see you hiding, you big hunk of bacon! That's not nice, playing tricks like that! Come here, Auntie Mali has some Cheerios for you."

"Peek- a- boo, I see you!" I grabbed a corner of the tarp and lifted it, fully expecting to see her lounging underneath the patio table and smirking at me. I was wrong.

"Crap. *Bazd meg!*" I let the Hungarian F-bomb equivalent fly from my mouth.

CHAPTER TWO

*N*ot again!

The object was black, like Chicha, but instead of being covered in fur, it was clothed. Black pants, black sweater, black winter boots, but no coat. A man lay crumpled in the corner of my garage, and a feeling of dread swept over me.

"Again?" I couldn't help but exclaim out loud. It hadn't even been a month since the last one. I fumed for a moment then instantly felt guilty for my momentary lack of compassion.

"Who're you talking to?"

I jumped at the voice. I hadn't heard Nora enter the garage. I quickly dropped the tarp back into place and rushed toward her. "I have some bad news, and some even worse news," I replied.

"Let's start with the worse news," Nora said cheerfully, as if I were about to tell her that she'd just won the lotto.

I hemmed and hawed a bit, then started with the news that I knew Nora would consider to be worse: "Chicha's missing. The door was slightly open; she must have wandered out."

"Oh, no! My poor girl, she'll be so distraught. She must

13

be hungry. We have to look for her now!" She whirled around and headed out of the garage. Before I could take two steps to follow her, she was back.

"What's the *other* bad news?"

"We have to call 911. There's a body here," I said simply.

I had thought she'd be upset, maybe even crumple to ground, so I was surprised when she started chattering. "Well, isn't this exciting? I can't believe I was here to see it this time. This is much more exciting than being at home with The Man. Where do we start, Mali?"

I shook my head, not quite believing what I was hearing. Maybe she was in shock. Yes, that had to be it, shock and grief over her missing pig and finding a corpse.

"Nora, are you all right? You're not going to faint or anything, are you?" I asked.

"Heck no! This is the most fun I've had in ages. I mean, it's not fun that this poor soul is dead in your garage, but you have to admit that this is exciting. Oh, do you think the murderer could be watching us right now?" She glanced about with her eyes sparkling, and struck a ninja pose, while I continued to shake my head. Perhaps I was the one in shock and imagining all this.

"We don't know that he's been murdered yet; I didn't take a close look. But it's definitely not good, and I can't imagine that he crawled under there for a nap. Why don't we go inside to warm up and call the cops?" She made a move toward the body but I grabbed her arm. "You don't want to see it, trust me." I was thankful but surprised that she took my word for it, albeit with a sigh of disappointment.

Back inside the bistro, I brewed a pot of extra strong coffee and we chatted while waiting for the police. I had called Matt, too, who'd groaned at the news and said he was on his way.

"I don't understand why you're so excited by all this, Nora?" I wondered. "I actually feel quite sick from it all."

"Are you kidding? Nothing ever happens at home. I can't remember the last time anything exciting happened in my life. I mean, as I said earlier, it's unfortunate that someone's dead in there, but maybe this time I can help you find the killer."

"Oh no, I am not getting involved again!" I exclaimed, subconsciously reaching up to my sore head. "Anyway, let's just wait to see what the cops say. Maybe the guy really is just sleeping. Or maybe he died of natural causes." I knew that was impossible after what I'd seen, but I was afraid that Nora would go rushing back into the garage for a look if I told her the truth.

"Did you take a pulse?" Nora asked.

"Um, no... He didn't look too good from what I saw." I thought it best not to mention the severely mangled eyeball.

Matt arrived within minutes and wrapped me in a big hug. "You are not getting involved this time," he ordered. "I almost lost you last time."

I sighed. He really shouldn't have said that.

On the one hand, I liked that he was being protective of me, but on the other... I had grown up under my parents' thumb and any time someone tried to tell me what to do, it was my nature to rebel. I was just hard-wired to do the opposite of what I was being ordered to do.

"It's not like I want to get involved. Maybe this time the cops will actually do something about it," I said hopefully. Truth be told, I wasn't quite up to playing the bumbling junior detective just yet.

Just then the cops arrived, and a moment later so did the ambulance that this poor man wouldn't need. To my horror, the first officer on the scene was Officer Sean. Yeah, *him*...

The same Officer Sean that had broken Nicole's heart by cheating on her. Or rather, he was cheating on his secret fiancé with Nicole. Any way I looked at it, I wasn't particularly happy to see the weasel.

15

"Sean..." I said through clenched teeth, purposely neglecting to address him as an 'Officer'. "Ma'am." he responded. He'd probably never bothered to learn my name. To his credit, he did shift around uncomfortably as I sneered at him.

"So, can you show me what you found?"

"This way," I snapped and stomped toward the garage with everyone following close behind. At the partially open door, I pointed, none too eager to go inside. "In there," I said.

The police looked around for a while, and not long after someone carrying a camera arrived to join them. Still later, the paramedics carried the man away. We watched from inside, since it was a balmy minus twenty Celsius outside. That's minus four Fahrenheit for our American friends. Welcome to January in Ottawa, the capital of Canada, one of the coldest capital cities in the world!

I hoped that they'd be done before Nicole arrived (although it would have been amusing to see what she would have done upon seeing Sean), and luckily they were. They joined us inside the bistro where I busied myself pouring coffee for everyone. My taste buds screamed for wine, but that would hardly be appropriate as it was just shortly after noon.

"I hope you won't have to shut down the bistro, since Saturday night is one of my busiest nights," I stated. Someone had just died and although it saddened me, I was forever cognizant of the fact that my bistro was my sole source of income. If it didn't do well, it was both my business and my home that I would lose.

"I don't think that's necessary, Ma'am, but we would like to take a quick look around in here. I have a team outside searching the grounds and the trails. Did you happen to notice any ski-dos in the area lately?"

Nora eagerly answered for me. "Oh, yes, there was a whole gang of them that stopped by here last night for Mali's ham and cheesy potato chowder. I noticed them when I was at the bar waiting for Nicole." This part Nora aimed in my direction, not realizing that this was the same Sean that Nicole had dated. However, with my eyes trained on Sean, I saw him wince at the mention of her name.

Good!

He nodded and then continued, "There's lots of ski-do tracks out there around your garage. Do you often get a ski-do crowd?"

"That was the first time, I think," I replied. "But don't forget, I only opened just over a month ago. There are trails next to my land though, and I'm pretty sure ski-doers and skiers and hikers use them often. Any clue how the man was murdered?" That question earned me a scowl.

"Ma'am, we've worked together before. You know I can't disclose very much. However, I'm sure you noticed the eye." I could feel Nora's eyes swing in my direction as I averted her gaze. "I'm sure you'll be reading about that in the newspaper." He nodded toward a news van that had just parked in my lot. "Excuse me." He went outside to join the news team, and after a brief statement, they left and he returned to his now lukewarm coffee. My natural kindness reacted instinctively and I took a bit of pity on the creep, topping it up for him with some hot brew, and he nodded his appreciation.

"Sean, do you think Mali's in any danger?" Matt spoke now, for the first time since Sean's arrival. Until now, he'd merely listened and observed.

"My guess would be no. Unlike the last time, this doesn't seem to be targeted toward Mali or the bistro in any way. An attempt was made to hide him, and with this cold weather, he would have been preserved for quite a while. What made you look back there?" Sean wondered as he turned to me. I noted a subtle shift in his tone and realized it was now time for me to make my statement.

"I was looking for Nora's pig." He raised his brows and I continued. "Nora's staying here for a little while and her pet pig was penned in the garage. I went out to feed her this morning and noticed that the side door to the garage was open. Chicha was nowhere to be found, but then I thought I saw something black peeking out from under the tarp and thought it was her. It was black, all right, but it wasn't the pig. Right then Nora arrived and then we called 911. I touched the tarp but nothing else, not even the door. I had pushed that in with my elbow." I was happy now that I'd listened to my tingling gypsy senses and had realized something was off kilter.

"I touched the door," Nora piped up. "I just pushed it in further with one hand...but I had mittens on." She held her hands up, showing off her red mitts that she was still wearing. Sean turned to face Matt. "I didn't go out there," he confirmed. At Sean's raised eyebrows, he elaborated, "I only got here minutes before you did." Sean raised his eyebrows further.

"Anything happen here last night?" Sean pressed. I almost blurted out that I wore a thong and Matt was about to drag me to his place before Nora had burst upon the scene but I was pretty sure this wasn't what Sean wanted to know, not officially, anyway. I snuck a peak at Matt and caught him sneaking a peak at me. We both smirked at each other.

"No, not that I know of, but my other friends, Nicole and Chloé were the ones working last night since I still have a concussion." His lips formed a thin line before asking me for a copy of yesterday's page from our reservation book (from previous experience, he knew I kept such a book) and for Chloé's number. We both knew he already had Nicole's number.

I made him a copy of the ledger, and to my surprise, two printed out. I must have hit the copy button twice by mistake. I brought it back to the table for him and noticed his team leaving the bistro and getting into their police cruisers.

"You can open today, but as I'm sure you can guess, the garage area is off limits. We've put up barriers and yellow tape defining a wide perimeter around it. It shouldn't affect your customer parking area, however, and I know I don't have to remind you not to discuss anything with your customers. We still have a team out on the trails, and you may see officers coming and going. We'll be in touch." With that, he was gone.

Yes, of course, I thought bitterly, just like last time. No matter, I'd find out what I needed to know from the town's people anyway, because in this town, word got around quickly.

CHAPTER THREE

*I*t was well past lunch by now so I fixed us a quick snack of thick slabs of mustard seed salami and slices of Irish Cheddar, Jalapeño Havarti and multigrain baguette. If I'm having a sandwich, I like my cold cuts sliced very thin, but when I'm just munching, I tend to like a thick cut.

We savored the aged cheddar made from cow's milk and infused with Irish Whisky. The nutty flavor married well with the grains in the bread and the saltiness of the salami. The bite of the Havarti took us by surprise. After a happy sigh I took a big swallow from my glass of Pinot Evil. Matt glared at me. "Is your head still hurting?" he asked, knowing full well I shouldn't be drinking yet.

"Yes. And the wine makes the Tylenol work much quicker," I snapped none too politely, taking another big swallow before pushing the glass away with another big sigh, this time not a happy one. He was right, of course; I shouldn't be drinking yet.

I turned to Nora. "By the way, why were you here so early this morning?" Now that we had a chance to relax, I noticed the dark circles underneath her eyes. Her face was normally very youthful, in stark contrast to her long silver hair. "Are you holding up okay?" I asked wondering if the day's events were too much for her and if she was regretting having left The Man.

"I'm bushed, to be honest. The morning wasn't exactly peaceful, but the night was even worse. I don't think we slept a wink. Nicole sure has some problems. Good thing I was there with her!" she exclaimed.

"You mean about the stalker...who's now in jail?" I wondered, confused.

"Yes, the stalker, but not the one in jail. There's a new one stalking her now!"

"What in the world are you talking about?" I asked, completely lost. My aneurism twitched again, throbbing slightly over my left temple. I was certain that the fact that it was always the left temple was significant. Of course, it's not really an aneurism—at least I don't think so—but that's what I call it, for lack of a better definition. I often experience a stabbing pain somewhere above my left eye that makes my entire face twitch for a few seconds. I should probably get it checked out, I thought to myself for the hundredth time.

"Apparently, someone else is after her now. Last night, her phone kept ringing and it was hang-up after hang-up, with the caller name and number blocked. It finally stopped around three in the morning, but just as we were about to fall asleep, there was loud banging on her door. But by the time we got to the door, whoever was there was gone. We couldn't settle down after that, so we drank another bottle of wine until our nerves settled. Would you mind if I went upstairs for a quick nap?"

"Sure, go on up. My parents are gone now, so I changed the sheets on the spare bed and there are clean towels in the linen closet. Just make yourself at home. You've got a few hours to relax," I assured her.

"Thanks, Mali. I know I barged in on you both yesterday. Now that I think about it, you were just about to go somewhere when I popped up, weren't you? You looked like you were in a hurry." She leaned back in her seat and looked from me to Matt, her eyes widening slightly and twinkling mischievously. "Hmmm, yes...sorry I ruined your night," she said with a smirk at our telltale blushes. I had to hand it to her, not much escaped her when she chose to take notice.

Blushing, I spoke quickly: "No worries. You go on up, and don't worry about a thing." Too tired to argue, she gave a final smirk then headed up through the inside stairway that led to my apartment.

When I had first moved in, my brother and I discovered the secret stairway that led from my office area on the main floor up to the living quarters, without having to use the outside stairs. It was handy, but I had to remember to keep it locked so my customers wouldn't accidentally wander up to my home. The former owners had barricaded the doors to the stairwell for that reason, but Stephen and I had uncovered them. This was also where a man had been murdered during a break-in when his partner had turned on him, so I was still always a little jumpy, not to mention sad, when that memory surfaced.

"Do you have plans for today?" I asked Matt.

He lips curved into a hopeful smile and he asked, "Do you want to pick up where we left off last night, now that your parents have left?"

I grinned. "I do, but first I have to get things started here. I know I'm not supposed to be working yet, but all I'm going to do is chop veggies and start the cooking—nothing strenuous. It's therapeutic. I'd love some help, though." With minimal convincing he agreed, and we set to work in the kitchen.

An hour later, I was up to my elbows in vegetables when I heard banging on the back door. Peering outside through the peephole, I saw that it was Nicole looking madder than a wet hen.

My back door has a story of its own, which is actually tied in with how generous my parents can be. It was previously just a normal door, as this had once been just a normal house, with a window that could open for a nice little breeze. But after a number of break-ins, and while I was recuperating in the hospital after nearly being killed by a maniac, my parents had installed a heavy steel door for my protection.

"Why didn't you just use your keys?" I asked Nicole.

"I forgot them at home. I had to speak to Officer Sean," she spat his name, "and after that I was flustered. You could have given me a heads-up, you know." I could tell she was miffed; she had every right to be. I'd been so flustered myself, and then so hungry that I'd completely forgotten to warn her. I apologized and then buttered her up with a chocolate treat, gaining forgiveness. She quickly recapped her conversation with him.

"So, did anything unusual happen here at the bistro last night?" Matt asked before I could.

"It was sort of a weird night, you could say. Nora had shown up with her pig, and there was a big ski-do gang here who'd already been drinking before they got here— they were pretty rowdy. Then, probably about an hour before we closed, a couple walked in, sat down near the piano area, and before I even had a chance to walk over to them, they got right back up and left in a rush. A guy sitting at another table took off after them, and then the lady that was with him ran out too. I was going to peek out the blinds to see what was going on but then your ex, Hans, walked in with some girl and sat over by the fireplace in the exact spot where you and Matt had been earlier, so I wanted to keep an eye on him."

"Hans? Here? With another woman? In *my* spot?" I asked incredulously. What nerve! Matt looked at me curiously.

She nodded. "They just had a drink and left. He didn't even speak to me, even though we've met a number of times before. Chloé served them, not knowing who he was, of course."

I took mental note of everything she described. I was surprised that I hadn't noticed any of this the night before, but then again, I had to admit that I'd been pretty focused on Matt, and then I had gone upstairs earlier than usual, too. It did irk me tremendously though that Hans had been served like he was a regular customer. He had no right to crash my place. But I pushed that thought aside for now.

"Were you okay, talking to Sean?" I asked gently. She snorted. "The snake had the nerve to ask me out again! He's trying to tell me she's just a friend, so when I asked him about the ring on her finger, he'd said it was just some ring she'd gotten from Avon. It wasn't a real diamond, and it wasn't from him, or so he claims. I just hung up on him after that, but he's texted me three times since then!"

"Are you sure you're feeling up to working tonight?" I asked, concerned.

"Yes, of course. I need to get rid of all this energy that I have right now," she insisted, shooing me out of the kitchen.

"Alright, well, we've got everything ready for tonight. Nora's upstairs napping, and Chloé should be here soon, so we're going to relax a bit. If you need anything, just let me know. I'll be upstairs." I grabbed Matts' hand and tugged gently for him to follow me. I felt suddenly worn out, the familiar crash and burn feeling when one of my thyroid pills wore off and it was time for another dose.

"So, do you have any plans for the rest of the day?" I asked again, this time on our way upstairs.

My intestines knotted in response to the sound of his husky voice as he reached for me in the stairwell and pulled me close. "No, other than hanging around to make sure that nothing else happens." Just as his mouth reached mine, the door at the top of the stairs opened and Nora appeared. Bless her soul, she had terrible timing.

"Hey, you two, get a room!" she cackled as she eased past us on her way downstairs. That's exactly what I'd like to do, I thought to myself.

I settled Matt on the couch then went into the kitchen and uncorked a bottle of red called Fourplay. With any luck, I planned to have some of that this evening. Fore-play, that is, not wine. Well, that too, if I could sneak some passed Matt and his hawk eyes.

As my friends already knew, I tended to choose wines that went with my mood, or with an event, or with my impressions of people. It kept me amused to no end. I laughed softly to myself over this particular choice of wine.

I downed a half a glassful to unwind, knowing full well I shouldn't be drinking yet and not caring, then topped up both glasses and joined Matt on the couch. I took a tiny, ladylike sip under his watchful eye to swallow my thyroid pill. He raised a brow.

"Hashimoto's hypothyroid," I explained. "I have to make sure I get plenty of rest as my energy can fizzle out pretty quickly. My doctor started me on this new pill not long ago that's supposed to give me a bit of an energy boost, but it only lasts about six to eight hours. And of course, if I'm not super careful, I gain weight very easily." I shrugged. "I've learned to adapt." It was a lie of course. I still hadn't adapted to my body betraying me, but I was hardly going to lay that on him this soon into our relationship. Instead, I changed the subject.

"If you don't mind, I'm going to take a quick shower. I hadn't gotten around to that yet when the day went downhill," I told him.

He grinned. "Call me if you need someone to wash your back!" I blushed and took another gulp from my glass. The relationship was still new so we weren't at the back washing stage yet, but I'd be lying if I said I wasn't tempted and that the thought of his soapy hands on me didn't send my blood pumping to sensitive areas. I hurried off before my mouth could decide to have a mind of its own.

26

CHAPTER FOUR

A quick shower with cucumber soap and a quick shave of all the necessary parts. Shampoo and conditioner, a nice sleek and shine brand with argon oils. What the heck, I thought, and lathered the conditioner all over my body too. If it was good enough for my hair, it would be good for my skin.

I dried my hair quickly, which meant I ended up with the wild tiger look, my natural caramel-colored waves going crazy now that they were unleashed. Normally, I would straighten my hair since I wasn't a fan of the kinky waves, but there wasn't time. I didn't want to keep Matt waiting. Next, a generous slathering all over with my new Bombshell lotion, followed by the matching body spray.

Definitely time to break in some of those new undies I had recently bought. I chose a soft yellow, silky bra and matching panties. Not a thong, but a very sexy cut that looked flattering, should anyone end up looking. Since we weren't venturing out, I put on some simple black yoga pants with a flowing black top. Casual, but cute and comfortable; I was all set. I quickly made the bed, since it was still in the nest position that I had left for Hummer earlier in the day. As I turned to leave the room, I was greeted by his eyes glaring at me. Clearly he was not impressed. I shrugged but did not offer an explanation.

Again, I joined Matt on the couch. Even after a busy day, he looked absolutely irresistible. I couldn't help but think of the country singer Keith Urban each time I looked at him, with his slightly longish sandy hair and blazing green eyes, tall, muscular body, wide and firm shoulders. In the few weeks that I'd known him, his hair had grown longer. I liked it.

Suddenly shy, I smiled and let my wild hair fall forward to partially cover the blush on my cheeks. He reached over to brush away the hair, drawing me close to him for a deep kiss.

"Nice look," he murmured his appreciation, playing with a tendril of my wavy hair. "And you smell fantastic," he purred as he drew me close. His tongue caressed mine as one hand gently ran up and down my back. The other hand was at the small of my back, with gentle pressure pushing me slightly forward until somehow I ended up on top of him on the couch. He moved his lips over my chin, toward my neck, tasting, kissing. My toes curled and my body flushed with anticipation.

"Wine?" I managed to choke, trying to sit up, suddenly nervous and not sure how quickly to allow this relationship to progress.

"No thank you," he answered, holding me firmly against him and kissing the hollow of my throat while a hand reached up and undid the top button of my shirt. My breath hitched and before I could stop them, my own hands reached underneath his shirt, caressing his chest, his shoulders.

He moaned and two more of my buttons came undone, his mouth traveling lower. "So pretty," I heard him say as he caught a peek at my bra. His lips found mine again and our tongues danced a little waltz. Oh, yes! Finally! Time alone! Oh, that was nice. Oh..."Amalia!"

Wha...oh...what? My mind couldn't make sense of anything.

"Amalia, hello?" Someone faraway said my name. "Oh, Mali, coming in!"

We leaped apart, feigning innocence as Nora's little face peered out from the kitchen. Yes... Bless her soul.

"Sorry to bother you, but I thought you'd be very interested in what I found out. Some customers mentioned that they knew who the person was that was murdered."

Matt and I both shot off the couch to join her. Belatedly, I realized my top was still partially undone. Nora pretended not to notice as I fumbled with the buttons, but I caught her playful smirk and knew that she'd comment later.

"Who?" we said in unison.

"You're not going to like this. And I'm sure it's going to make your life more difficult..."

"Nora, spit it out already!" I urged impatiently.

"It's Mr. Leonardo's nephew." Matt and I both gasped. She was right; this wasn't good news.

Mr. Leonardo is my nemesis. He owns the pizza place in the town of Robin where the Whine is located, the only other place to eat other than my bistro, unless you're cooking for yourself. He'd had a feud with the previous owners, which I suspected was actually a cover since it turned out he was sleeping with Harriet, the wife of the former owner.

He had taken an instant dislike to me and had even thrown a bat of pepperoni at me when I went to try to make friends with him. If his nephew turned out to be the body in my garage, it certainly wasn't good news. I groaned in frustration and headed for the fridge. Ferreting out a wedge of marbled cheddar, I contemplated this turn of events.

"What else are the customers saying? Do we know if he was with the ski-do crowd that night?" I chomped into the cheese ferociously, holding it personally responsible for the events of the day.

"That's all I know right now, but I'll get back down there and pump them!" Nora's eyes were flashing with excitement. She was clearly enjoying this. "Afterward, though, can we check the trails for Chicha? I know the cops were out there and didn't see her, but I'd like to try, too."

"Nora, we can't cross the crime scene tape to get to the trails," I reminded her gently.

"But there is another way," Matt said. "We can park down by Joey's house and get to the trails from his property."

Brilliant! Matts' dearly departed friend Joey had a house that was directly across the trails from my own.

We agreed to meet in an hour. By that time, Nicole and Chloé could manage without Nora and me inside the bistro. Matt and I gathered flashlights and some food for Chicha then sat down to wait for Nora. I was about to take a sip of wine when I noticed the little wet paw prints across my glossy white Ikea coffee table. Oh, Hummer. I should have known better than to leave an unattended glass within his reach.

We dumped our wine down the sink and Matt pulled me close. "This is better than wine, anyway," he whispered as his lips claimed mine. My hands snaked around his neck and... "Hey, sorry I'm late!" Bless her soul. We jumped apart again.

"We've got everything set Nora. Let's go; it's getting pretty late." We set off in Nora's van, just in case we did find Chicha and had to bring her back.

"I found out a little bit more from the customers," Nora offered. "His name is Alphonso Brut, Alfie for short. He was married, but word around town is that he was having an affair, and probably not his first. People say he was even nastier than Mr. Leonardo and that you didn't mess with Alphie. When I asked what they meant by that, they'd just repeat it and wink."

Could it be that our little town of Robin had their own Mafia? It was hard to believe, if that was the implication.

"Oh, and in answer to your question earlier, yes, he was really into ski-doing. I didn't find out if he was with the ski-do crowd though, but chances are he knew them. But more interesting than that, word is that even Mr. Leonardo didn't like his own nephew. Now that has to be good news for you!"

The wheels in my brain were spinning. I had to get this ski-do crowd back into my bistro somehow and ask some questions. And I had to find out why Mr. Leonardo hated his own nephew. I groaned inwardly. I was getting involved again, wasn't I? But in my defense, I just hated it when someone ended up dead on my property.

We arrived at Joey's house and set off exploring the trails, peering into the dark forest all around us with the flashlights. But there was no sign of Chicha, nor any evidence of hoof prints, although it was hard to tell at this time of night. It had started to snow and that was making it more challenging. And it didn't take long for our voices to grow hoarse from repeatedly calling the pigs' name.

After an hour, we decided to head back, vowing to set out again in daylight. Nora left a trail of Cheerios leading back toward Joey's house and fought to hold back her tears. I reached out and gave her a hug. "We'll find her, Nora; don't you worry." She nodded and sniffled.

"Damn, my tears are turning into icicles in this cold," she tried to joke. "Let me just get the blankets out of the van and put them down out here somewhere. Maybe if she follows the trail of Cheerios I left for her, she'll find the blankets to stay warm."

We made a nice bed just at the mouth of the trail for Chicha and left the last of the box of Cheerios and some vegetables. For Nora's sake, I hoped the little porker would be okay.

CHAPTER FIVE

By the time we got back, the bistro was closed and Nicole and Chloé were finishing tidying up. "Would you like to come upstairs for a bit?" I asked. "I have a bottle of Inniskillin Ice Wine that I've been dying to taste." Even I involuntarily winced at my poor choice of wording.

Everyone agreed and we all trudged upstairs, weary after a long and eventful day. They sat in the living room chatting while Matt poured the ice wine and I assembled some mini vanilla sponge cakes that I'd bought days earlier to which I added strawberry topping.

Ice wines are categorized as a dessert wine and are made from grapes that have been frozen while still on the vines, which results in a concentrated sweetness in the grape. There's a fairly small amount of ice wine made world-wide, and as a result it tends to be quite pricey. This particular bottle from Ontario cost fifty dollars, so we savored each sip.

And yes, it was scrumptious! I could taste peach, brown sugar and a hint of apricot, and it paired wonderfully with the strawberry shortcake. The room fell quiet, interrupted only with an occasional sigh of contentment.

Once finished, we made feeble attempts at small talk. "Any sign of Chicha?" Chloé asked hopefully. Nora shook her head, her cheeks suddenly appearing as though they were drooping. With her youthful attitude and smooth skin, I would often forget that she was in her mid-fifties, even despite her silver hair. Now, suddenly, she looked her age.

"Have you heard from Sean?" I asked Nicole.

"Officer Sean," she spat his name again, "has texted me eight times today. The Sean I met the other day also texted, and I'll be seeing him tomorrow for brunch." At the end of her relationship with Sean, Nicole had met another Sean, one of Matts' body guards, who so far seemed very nice. With two Sean's in the picture, it was getting confusing.

"Isn't Officer Sean married?" Matt asked, confused.

"He says that they were seeing each other for a time, and that she is now just a roommate and is now looking for another place to stay. I don't believe any of it though, and I told him to get lost, but it's just making him more determined." Nicole's eyes flashed in anger.

"What are we going to do about the murder?" Nora asked impatiently, tiring of the chit-chat and finally bringing up the real reason we had gathered.

"I have an idea..." I got no further before Matt threw up his hands in frustration. The sudden resemblance to my father was uncanny, and more than a little unnerving.

"You can't do this Amalia. Do you want to get killed this time?" He glowered at me.

"Hear me out, Matt. It doesn't involve me," I replied sweetly, although inside I was bristling. Hadn't he figured out yet that I did not react well to being told what to do? I pushed the feeling aside, for now, and continued with my plan. "Mr. Leonardo's never seen Nora before. I'm thinking maybe Nora should go into his shop, order a pizza, and offer her condolences to see where it goes from there. Maybe she can find out something about the nephew. That is, if she feels comfortable doing something like that..." My voice rose as I looked at Nora hopefully.

Nora sat up, ramrod straight and suddenly re-energized. "Oh, yes! I love it! And I could go for a pizza, too!"

It was a weak plan and dependent entirely on luck, but it was somewhere to start. And I had to admit, I really wanted to taste Leonardo's pizza. I hated being ostracized, and at this point the pizza was like forbidden fruit. I suppose I could understand if I had done something to upset him, but the man hated me merely for the fact that I was his only competition in town, even though we didn't serve the same type of food. Go figure!

"Okay, whoever wants pizza, come back to the bistro tomorrow afternoon. We'll get an extra-large one so there will be plenty for everyone. And one more thing; if we can switch our focus to business for just a moment, Valentine's Day is less than a month away. We need to design a couple of new t-shirts, so I need ideas."

We had decided to dress simply and comfortably in a black skirt or pants at the bistro, but I also liked to get custom tunic-style tees made featuring something cheeky on it about one of our wines, usually in black and red to go with the bistro's theme of black and red decor. The tunics were both comfortable and flattering to all body shapes, and best of all, they required no ironing, which was perfect for someone who didn't know how to iron—someone like me!

"You have a wine called Passion, right?" said Matt. "How about something like 'Tonight is a night for Passion'?" We unanimously agreed that we liked the suggestion. It was perfect for Valentine's Day and I'd have to remember to showcase some of those bottles in my glass display cabinet of items available for purchase to take home and to continue the passion there. I stole a quick glance in Matt's direction. Was he hoping for a night of passion with me?

"I have one," said Nora. "People get frisky on Valentine's Day, right? How about that Frisky Zebras that you have from South Africa? If I remember correctly, the label describes it as a seductive Shiraz."

"Yes, I'm getting an idea from that...almost... yes, I love it! It would have to be black and white though, but that would still match the place quite nicely. We can have the shirts done in the zebra colors and maybe have a big red heart somewhere and written inside it the caption, "Are you feeling Frisky? Yes, that could work." I did some quick sketches that were laughable since I'm not talented in any way. But I knew that the t-shirt guy would get the idea and be able to work his magic.

Nicole and Chloé both left and Nora went out to look around the house one last time, hoping that Chicha had returned. I walked Matt to the door and gave him a long kiss, promising we'd find time alone eventually. "Are you coming tomorrow for pizza?" I asked.

"I have some things to do, but I'll definitely be here later. Are you attempting to work tomorrow?"

"Yes. My friends have helped me so much and I'm feeling very guilty. I'm pretty sure my concussion is okay now. I didn't have any headaches today, and I'll take it slow. Come over any time though; I'll feed you something home cooked, or maybe Mr. Leonardo's pizza, if you're lucky."

"How about Schnitzel?" he asked hopefully. Damn, my mother had spoiled him with her cooking when she was here last week. Everyone fell under the spell of her almighty schnitzel.

"No, I think I'll be making stuffed pasta shells with homemade creamy garlic sauce and loaded with a medley of melted cheeses." My mouth was already watering as I envisioned the dish. Matt brought me back to reality the moment his lips made contact with mine.

We kissed a last lingering kiss, yet not daring to get too involved since we knew Nora would return any second.

Sure enough, he'd no sooner gone out the door when it opened again and Nora trudged inside, covered in snow and wiping her eyes.

"We'll find her, Nora, even if we have to call everyone in town for help," I assured her and gave her another hug before we each went off to our rooms and crawled into bed.

MINI STRAWBERRY SHORTCAKES

Quick version:
- Ready-made mini cakes, often in the fruit section at your grocery store
- Package of strawberries, cleaned, hulled and sliced
- Tub of thawed cool whip (I always use light or fat free)

Unwrap cakes, top with a layer of cool whip and a layer of strawberries and another layer of whipped cream. Place a strawberry on top as a "hat". If you feel like getting fancy, replace first layer of whipped cream with a layer of vanilla or banana flavored pudding or custard.

Complicated version: Buy a package of biscuit mix and make biscuits according to package directions, allow to cool then layer whipped cream and strawberries as outlined above.

More complicated version: Make mini cakes or biscuits from scratch. You can google or Pinterest for recipes as I try not to get overly complicated if I can avoid it.

CHAPTER SIX

*I*t was a lazy Sunday morning. Nora didn't budge from her room until almost ten, and I was enjoying my coffee in bed and watching The Pioneer Woman on the Food Network channel when I finally heard her stir. We grunted at each other, neither of us morning people, and I whipped up a quick, very small breakfast, since in a couple of hours we'd be eating pizza. After we ate, we headed out to her van to drive over to Joey's place to look for Chicha again.

Although Joeys' house was only a few miles down the road from my own, the drive seemed to take forever. Traffic was backed up and hardly moving, which was very unusual for the town of Robin, and in particular for a Sunday. Although this was the main road in this rural town, traffic is only heavy if there's been an accident, which is rare, or if there was an issue with the train track signal for the tracks that cross the main road. The drive from the beginning of Robin Road to my bistro usually took a total of seven minutes.

After an agonizing twenty minutes, we finally passed the house with the goat that was always sitting outside on a wooden table. Normally, I would be passing by this house

41

within a minute of having left mine. Harold the goat, as I had named him in my head, was at his usual post.

We were still about two miles away when we happened upon the cause of the delay. Nora was the first to see it and abruptly pulled over to the shoulder of the road and jumped out of the van before I could react. I watched as she ran ahead a few paces waving her arms as if she were fighting off a swarm of bees, and then fell to knees. My first thought was that she'd had a heart attack, but then, with relief, saw her throwing her arms around Chicha, who was out for a stroll. Country living at its finest!

I too jumped out of the van. Nora was crying with relief, and I broke out in tears as well. I admit freely that I cry just from seeing others cry. The drivers around us honked, either from sharing our joy or to tell us to get the hell off the road.

Nora stood with Chicha while I returned to the van and slowly drove along the shoulder until I reached them. I still didn't know how we were going to get the pig inside the vehicle, but Nora soon solved that problem. She opened the back of the van and slid the ramp into position. Seeing her tiny body at work made me realize that I should never underestimate this woman. We pushed and prodded and bribed Chicha with Cheerios until she was up the ramp and safely inside the back of the van, then we took her home. Since the garage was still off limits, we brought her to the back of the house. While Nora coddled the pig, I drove back to Joey's house to retrieve the blankets we had left there the night before.

But I froze when I saw that the blankets weren't empty. I was about to turn and run, but he spotted me at the same time and shouted, "Hey! Thanks for the food and the blankets!"

Sensing no immediate danger, I turned cautiously and studied him. He looked vaguely familiar but I couldn't quite place him.

"I sure wish you'd left a sandwich, though. Man, that

was good the other day!"

Ding-dong! I had been admiring my newly installed back door when he'd burst in, demanding money. I had offered him a sandwich instead, and although he wasn't thrilled, he'd grabbed it and ran. I now make sure that door is locked. But what a strange world this is! It was stranger still, imagining him eating the trail of Cheerios that we'd left for Chicha.

I waved but didn't engage in conversation. I went back to the van. I didn't need him following me home and hanging around the bistro like a stray cat.

Back home, I rustled up some sheets and another blanket, none of them old, so they would need to be replaced. Since we couldn't use my garage yet, Nora and I made a makeshift tent outside, a few feet away from the house. The weather was mild, so the snow from the day before was melting and dripping off the roof. The crude shelter would have to do until we could get our hands on a real tarp or use the garage again.

This time, Chicha was chained like a dog so she couldn't escape. Nora had thought to bring the chain the day she'd moved in, but it was a shame that she hadn't used it the first night. Of course, we never figured the door would be left open, either.

We were just wrapping up when Officer Sean rounded the corner and joined us. He noted the pig and nodded, then jumped in surprise when she sneezed. "She has a cold," Nora explained. "Mali, do you have any turkey?" The pig ate turkey?

"Uh, no. But I have some chicken. Chicha eats poultry?"

"Not usually, but when she gets a cold, I make her turkey soup. Mind if I use the chicken to make it?"

"If you're inclined to make a big pot, then we can put it on the menu for tonight. That'll be less work for me!" She nodded and headed off, leaving me with Sean.

Sean was normally a pretty boy and reminded me of my

ex, Hans, who preened more than I ever had, got his hair done more than I ever did and spent more on clothes than I would ever bother to spend. Today, though, Sean had dark circles underneath his blue eyes. Hans would never have allowed himself to be seen in public like that.

"Sorry about what happened with Nicole," he stammered. "It was all a misunderstanding. That's not why I'm here, though." He'd abruptly changed the subject and I was left wondering why he felt compelled to bring up Nicole and how he'd cheated on her. "We're going to have a team here shortly for another look inside the garage. We've identified the man," I nodded and he nodded in return, realizing I already knew. "The murder weapon wasn't found, of course. That would make our jobs too easy. But we know it was something long and about two inches wide. It went in through his eye and cut right through his brain, so he probably died quickly." He noted my wince and apologized. "You'll hear this through the grape-wine here in Robin, so you might as well hear it from me first. We can't figure out what it was, but at least we have an idea of the shape. I have a tent you can have for the pig, if you like. I don't use it anymore." The abrupt change in conversation again left me unsettled.

"Sure. Please." I was too flustered for complete sentences. As unexpectedly as he'd arrived, he whirled round and left. I went inside to help Nora with the soup since it was time for her to call on Mr. Leonardo.

CHAPTER SEVEN

"Okay, Nora, it's show time," I announced. "I'll finish the soup for you while you go to get a pizza. Oh, by the way, Officer Sean will be bringing us a tent for Chicha."

She looked at me, startled. "Well, that's awfully nice. I wonder if there's any truth to his story and that that woman really was just his roommate?"

I shook my head. "No, when I saw them enter that bar together last week, he definitely had his arm around her in a boyfriend kind of way. I don't buy the nice guy act."

She went up to her room to get cleaned up and then drove over to Leonardo's. By one o'clock in the afternoon, I was starting to worry. I had expected her back half an hour ago. I tried her cell phone but it went immediately to voice mail. "This day just keeps getting weirder," I said out loud to myself.

She finally bustled in an hour later, her cheeks flushed with excitement. "Boy, oh boy, that was fun!" she exclaimed.

"What took you so long? I was starting to worry." I looked at her expectantly and her flushed cheeks seem to grow even more flushed. "Did something happen? Did

45

you find out something?"

"Mr. Leonardo sure is handsome," she giggled.

I dropped the ladle I'd been using to stir the meat mixture for my stuffed pasta shells. "What?"

"I was placing my order at the front when he looked out from the kitchen. He came right over to me, took my hand, kissed it, and said something that sounded very romantic in Italian. Of course I didn't understand. But I think I have a date for tonight..."

I shook my head. Perhaps I had narcolepsy and had fallen asleep and had had a bad dream. "The man hates me, Nora! How could you go out with him?"

"Well, he doesn't know that I know you. Anyway, now I can pump him for information. I'm going there around eight for dinner."

Nora brought some soup out to Chicha then helped me in the kitchen with the pasta. At opening time, when Nicole and Chloé arrived, Nora left for her date. If I were completely honest, I would have to confess that I felt a little betrayed.

"How'd your date with the New Sean go?" I asked Nicole, brushing my troubled thoughts aside.

She shrugged. Was she losing interest already?

"He's a real sweetheart but he's...clingy. He never wants our dates to end and calls a few times a day, which would be great, I guess, but the spark is just not there for me." She paused and I sensed that there was more. "Someone's stalking me...maybe it's him."

This day was definitely getting weirder by the minute.

"Someone showed up at my apartment door during the night and left flowers and chocolates," she continued. "I threw it all away. You never know if someone's going to sneak poison onto something..." She shuddered and a chill went down my own spine. "There wasn't a note, and I was getting weird calls with the caller ID blocked all night. Whoever it is sure likes the sound of my breathing. I stopped answering after a while, and then they just breathed onto my voicemail."

"Do you think it's him?" I asked.

"I almost hope it is. That thought is more comforting than the thought that somebody out there is stalking me."

We were in full swing serving customers when Matt walked in with his pal and co-worker, Ricky. Ricky was a bug-eyed looking guy and had been on the police force with Matt until a gunshot wound had nearly ended his life. Both quit the force soon after that. Matt had moved out west and returned two years later, opening his private eye and security guard company, where Ricky also now worked as Matt's second in command.

To my horror, and to Nicole's, Officer Sean also decided to drop by. He sat alone at the bar, eating Nora's soup and watching Nicole's every move. Luckily, by then our rush was dying down, so I sent her to the kitchen to prep plates while Chloé and I served the clients.

As I stood before him, he asked for another glass of wine. Noting that he was drinking red, I poured him a glass of Plungerhead and smirked. I immediately felt a tinge of guilt when he told me that he'd brought Chicha the tent and had erected it outside. We were saved from further conversation when a group of ski-doers arrived, all of them asking for a hearty bowl of soup after a day in the snow. I studied them carefully and perked up my ears, hoping to catch a snippet of conversation. I wasn't disappointed.

"It's always about which trail he wants to go on and what he wants to do. I'm surprised no one has run him over with a ski-do," said a burly guy wearing heavy snow pants. "Today was a lot more fun without him, and I know you all agree even if you're too nice to say so." A few heads bobbed in agreement while others diverted their eyes.

On my scratchpad, I briefly noted what he'd said and jotted down a quick description: tall, fat, beard, dark hair, brown eyes... "C'mon, Markus, he's dead, so get over it."

Name: Markus. The two men glared at each other. I glanced at Officer Sean, but he was too far away from the group to have overheard anything, and besides, I saw that he was settling his bill with Chloé and preparing to leave.

The men were eating in silence, so I ambled over, intent on stirring things up a little. "Hello. I couldn't help overhearing. I'm so sorry for your loss." A dozen eyes first swung my way then looked nervously at Markus.

"He was a mean bastard, really. He claimed to have connections, and he always held that over our heads so we'd do what he wanted us to do."

"Why did you invite him to join you?" I wondered.

"We didn't invite him. We'd meet in the parking lot at the corner, near the pizza place, and he picked up on that and just started showing up. We meet every Friday at six at night during the winter, and on Saturdays and Sundays at nine a.m. Hey! You want to ride along some time?" I resisted the urge to gag when I saw droplets of soup in his gnarly beard.

"Oh, thanks for the invite, but unfortunately, those are my busiest days here, so I could never get away," I politely declined then got the conversation back on track. "You know, I've heard various stories... And of course I'm interested, because this *is* my place... And, as you probably know, this *isn't* the first time... So, I was just wondering, is it true that he was married and cheating on his wife?" I watched Officer Sean's back as he exited the bistro. What kind of cop didn't even realize that the very people he probably needed to question were sitting right under his eyes?

Again, a dozen eyes swung in my direction. Markus's back stiffened momentarily as he devoted his attention to his soup. Slowly, he looked up at me and studied me shrewdly, then nodded. "For a new gal in town, you know your stuff, don't you? I told the cops this yesterday, you know, that he never came with us on Friday nights. That was probably his night with the girlfriend. We'd just

48

arrived here on Friday night when we saw him leaving." He looked me up and down. "You wouldn't happen to be the apple of his eye, would you?"

I was taken aback by the question. Matt came to my rescue by tapping me on the shoulder and then giving me a quick kiss. "I'll be outside," he said, and I knew he was up to something.

I turned back to Markus, blushing from Matt's public display of affection. "I guess you can see that you've got that all wrong," I said. He offered me another ride on his machine, but of course I wasn't interested. I asked Chloé to take over the table the rest of the night.

So, the police had talked to some of the snowmobilers already. And perhaps that explained Officer Sean's lack of interest. But one thing that Markus said had stuck in my mind and kept replaying itself like an old record with a skip. It was just past closing time and I was wondering where Matt was, when the missing link clicked into place.

Markus had said that Alphie was just leaving when the ski-do crowd got here, and that he was never with them on Friday nights, so he'd likely come here by car. However, when I found the body on Saturday morning, there was no car in my lot. Whoever he was with had either driven the car away, or he was killed elsewhere and then dumped here. My musings were interrupted when Nora entered through the rear door. She was grinning like a Cheshire cat, and we gathered around her and waited to hear about her date with Mr. Leonardo.

"What a sexy man! He's such a good kisser." I gagged audibly and almost dropped the dishes I was holding.

"You kissed him?" I shouted. "How could you kiss him?" Almost predictably, my aneurism trembled in dismay.

"Sorry, Mali, it just sort of happened. I've been with Craig for so long now that I didn't remember what it was like to kiss someone else. What's the point of being separated if I don't have a little fun?"

"Can't you have fun with someone else? Anyone else? Everyone else, for that matter, except him?" I knew that I could probably fix her up with Markus.

She shrugged. "He'll do for now. Anyway, don't you want to know what I found out?"

I harrumphed my consent. I was dying of curiosity. "Before you start, I'm starving. Hold that thought." I quickly fixed a plate with some black pepper-seed salami, some parmesan-wrapped, red wine-infused salami, and pieces of Irish Cheddar, along with thin slices of buttery Asiago (another recent favorite). I also grabbed a package of garlic bagel chips and headed back to join the girls. Someone had poured each of us a glass of Goats do Roam, and I snickered. Around here, it should be Pigs do Roam, I thought to myself. Or perhaps old ladies do roam...

"Alright; let's hear it," I said, now in better spirits because I was munching. And I would apparently just have to get used to Nora's newfound libido.

"Well, I'll leave out the juicy parts, but I brought the conversation around to his nephew, pretending I'd overheard something at the corner store. He knew all about his nephew cheating on his niece, who is his favorite niece, by the way, and that's why he hated Alphie. Leo had confronted him about the affair a number of times, but Alphie just laughed at him and threatened to cut him down at the knees, saying he had connections. Leo didn't know if he did or if he didn't, but didn't want to find out either."

"So, if he had connections, then maybe he pissed someone off and they took him out," I suggested. "Do we know if his wife knew about the affairs?"

Nora shook her head. "I asked Leo that," she said proudly. "He didn't think so. Everyone in the family who knew tried to keep her sheltered from the news. She might have heard the rumors around town though. I mean, it's pretty hard not to."

"How about the girlfriend? Does anyone know who

she was?" Chloé asked while slipping off her six-inch heels and stretching her calves. That girl had a serious shoe collection.

"Leo didn't know, but that doesn't mean others didn't. We'll have to dig around some more. I can ask around at the local stores tomorrow," she volunteered. I gladly accepted. The local merchants didn't like having me as a customer as they all feared losing Mr. Leo's business since his disdain of me was so public.

As if she read my mind, Nora spoke again: "I mentioned the bistro to him. I just asked if he'd ever eaten here and it was like his blood pressure rose right before my eyes. I asked him why he was upset and he just shut me down. He said he didn't want to talk about *that place*, as he put it. I'll keep chipping away at him, though."

Our little party broke up and as Nicole and Chloé were leaving, I noticed Nicole peak out the blinds and scan the area. It was reminiscent of a few weeks ago, when we were both on edge and both being followed. "Are you going to be okay, Nicole?" I called out. She nodded then darted out to her car. I locked the front door behind her and then Nora and I headed up to our beds.

My cell phone had died so after plugging it in to recharge it, I found Matt's text. He had decided to follow Markus and would be in touch the next day. My gypsy senses were tingling and I could feel that we were on to something. Of course, according to my parents I'm not really a gypsy, but I don't know if I believe them. I often get vague feelings, prescient feelings, but admittedly my gypsy senses seem to fail me when I need them most. Maybe I am only part gypsy.

Regardless, I am convinced there is gypsy blood in my background somewhere, and maybe I just have to figure out how to be more in touch with those sensations. I have vowed to track down our heritage one day, just to prove my parents wrong. In the meantime, speaking of my parents, they had left a voicemail for me to call them, but it was too late now. Whatever it was would have to wait until morning.

I rolled over and snuggled with Hummer, who was happily purring in the crook of my arm. I was having a dream that I was eating all my favorite foods (my favorite dream, by the way) when something clicked in my brain and woke me. I sat straight-up in bed, sending Hummer scattering with a yowl.

Another missing link had found its place.

CHAPTER EIGHT

*M*onday morning. The place was so quiet that I could hear Hummer snoring at the end of my bed. At first I thought my asthma was acting up, and that I was wheezing, until I held my breath and just listened. Hearing the sounds continue, I was able to narrow it down to my kitty deep in sleep. I smiled and relished the moment.

Since it was Monday, Nora was gone to her day job at an insurance company where I, too, used to work what now seemed like a lifetime ago, and I was off for three days. Currently, the bistro was only open Thursday's to Sunday's. Sometimes I would open on other nights for special events, such as Men's' Monday, or when my cash flow dictated it.

My calm was soon interrupted when the phone shrilled. Call display confirmed that it was my parents. "*Szia*" I answered in Hungarian. *Szia* is like the Italian *Ciao*, and means both hello and good bye.

"*Szerbusz*, Amalia, *hogy vagy*?" Hi, how are you?

"Hey mom; hey dad!" As always, both were on the line, each speaking loudly. "How's everything?"

"Great news! We're going to start moving tomorrow.

Would you be able to get the key for us today?"

My breath caught in my throat and the muscles in my face puckered in dismay. I'd thought I had two more weeks of freedom before they moved from Montreal. *Le sigh*... "Yes, of course. But, why the rush?" And why, oh why, did they have to come just as there was another murder that hasn't been solved yet, and that I hadn't told them about?

"Well, the weather's going to be good for the next few days, so we figured we'd take advantage of it. There's no problem getting the key early since the house is empty and the former owners have already moved out of the country. We just have to sign a waiver clearing them of any responsibility if something goes wrong before the official move date. So we'll also need you to take a look around the house and make sure everything's okay for us."

"No problem. I have to go into town today anyway, so I can swing by the realtor's office. Is Stephen coming too?"

"Yes, your brother is here now helping us with the packing and to load the moving van."

We hung up and I heaved myself out of bed as though the world rested on my shoulders and feeling woefully sorry for myself. My freedom would soon cease to exist. I sent my brother a quick text. "Sucker!" He had to spend the entire day and the next with them. He replied almost immediately "Soon they're all yours". Touché. He'd won this round.

I sighed again. I love my parents dearly, and they are wonderful, generous people. But did I mention smothering? Despite my love for them, I had been thrown for a loop when they had announced that they were moving to Ottawa.

The problem is that whenever they ware around, I felt as though I've reverted to being a child rather than a grown woman. I move from confident business woman to insecure child in the blink of an eye. It was no wonder that such lack of control had led to five years of anorexia in my teens until, just before my twentieth birthday, I moved out of their house and moved in with Hans. Pushing my bleaker thoughts aside, I reminded myself that my parents only wanted me to succeed and to be happy. Whatever my issues were, they were mine to battle and to overcome.

I drove into town, picked up the key from the realtor and then zipped by one of my favorite shops in the west end of Ottawa in an area called Kanata. *Just Cheese* was a specialty shop that sold over two hundred different cheeses. I bought many cheeses wholesale from there for the bistro, and as such, I enjoyed free delivery, but it was more fun to shop in person. I filled my basket and couldn't resist buying a little wedge of 'Stinking Bishop', voted one of the most pungent cheeses from the UK. I wouldn't likely be tasting it myself, due to my extreme gag reflex, but I knew it would sell at the bistro, and at the very least be good for a laugh.

They didn't have my favorite Irish Cheddar, however, which was proving to be a popular seller.I grinned as the owner mentioned an influx of recent customers looking for that cheese after tasting it at a bistro. I placed an order and was assured that they would deliver it once it was in stock again. The owner grinned upon realizing that I was the owner of said bistro.

Next, I rushed into the grocery store and rushed through in record time, grabbing whatever I thought my parents would need within the next few days. As I was leaving the store and easing the mini shopping cart onto the paved parking lot, I suddenly found myself airborne. Without understanding what had just happened, I discovered that all four of my limbs were flailing in the air as I perched on my stomach on top of the overturned cart. To my horror, I could not seem to make contact with the ground, and the searing pain was beginning to register. I can only imagine what I must have looked like, with my arms and legs flapping uselessly.

Two young guys rushed to my aid, easing me off the

cart and gently to my feet. The pain shot down my legs and I buckled over slightly.

"Are you okay ma'am?" one of them asked, shocked and concerned. The blush in my cheeks blazed but even worse than that, he had called me the dreaded 'ma'am'!

"Yes, thank you. I have no clue how that happened," I managed to reply. The pain in my legs was incredible. I made a move to pick up the scattered groceries and could barely move. The two men scrambled to reload my cart for me and asked again if I was alright before I hobbled away, clutching the cart for support.

I slowly pushed my way to the car, wincing with every step. I loaded the groceries into the car before daring to look at my legs.

The front of both had taken the brunt of my fall, the skin now broken and bleeding. Leaving my pants rolled up, I shakily got into the car and took a few moments to dab at my injuries with a tissue. Even if I don't look for trouble, it seems to find me.

I stopped by my place first to drop off the cheeses and to collect some cleaning supplies and my vacuum cleaner. I covered my injuries with a number of extra-large bandages, took a couple of Tylenols and then continued on to my parent's new house. There was no time to wallow in self-pity.

I hobbled about, cleaning corners and stocking their fridge. I vacuumed the entire house. I thought some flowers might make a nice greeting, so I took my chances and headed over to the corner grocery store for a bouquet.

I peeked inside to see who was at the cash till. A young girl with her hair in a bun; I was safe. If I didn't know her, then she didn't know me, which meant I could make a purchase without being shooed out, like last time. It was true that Mr. Leonardo had his thumb on this town, and everyone in it was afraid of his wrath, so they didn't want to be caught with me inside their shops, which really irked me.

I limped inside, found some flowers then hastened to the till as quickly as I could. I didn't want to push my luck by lingering. Before me were two other customers waiting in line, discussing the murder. Of course my ears perked up.

"Now, all we have to do is get rid of his uncle and this town can breathe easier," one man joked. The cashier's head snapped up and she glared at him, but it went unnoticed.

"He sure was nasty. When he worked for Leonardo, he messed up our pizza order once and when my husband complained, he spat on the pizza!" the lady behind him said. "They got into a brawl and they both came out of it black and blue. We never went back there after that. It sure is nice having another restaurant here in town now."

I let my long hair fall slightly over my face to make sure she didn't recognize me, but felt a swell of pride at the mention of the Whine and Cheese.

"Well, he'd been working at the post office for the past year now and I'm sure he snooped through the mail. Some friends of mine from Quebec had mailed me a gift card at Christmas that I never received. I'm sure he pocketed it, but I could never prove it. I even went in to ask about it and he threatened to cut me off at the knees. I won't miss him, let me tell you." His face darkened in anger as he shared his story.

"I know someone that he had a relationship with years ago, one affair of many, I know for certain," the lady said in a low voice this time. "When he offered to get her husband out of the picture, she ended it and then put her house up for sale. I don't know how his wife put up with him..." Her voice faded as they walked out together. I smiled sweetly, paid for the flowers and was just about to leave when my mouth opened and words tumbled out. Would the owner of this mouth please step forward?

"Did Mr. Brut live here in Robin? I mean, everyone around here seemed so afraid of him." I said to the cashier.

She opened up to me immediately.

"Yes, he was in the subdivision right behind us here. His family is still there, of course, and they come in here often. I'm just happy they weren't in here now to overhear those people. His wife is the sweetest thing."

I nodded politely and shuffled out. It was a successful mission, and I had found out that Mrs. Brut lived in the same subdivision my parents were moving to.

NORA'S CHICKEN SOUP

- 4 chicken thighs with bones and skin or the leftovers from last night's chicken dinner.
- 1 chopped onion, any kind, any size
- 1 small chopped green and/or red pepper
- 3 large peeled carrots chopped whatever size you like- I like mine in big chunks
- 3 stalks of celery, diced
- 1 sweet potato (yam) peeled, chopped
- 2 small turnips, peeled, chopped
- 4 good sized potatoes peeled and chopped
- 1 cup finely chopped frozen or fresh spinach
- 10 cups water or chicken broth (if using chicken broth, don't add salt unless needed)
- 1 teaspoon salt- add more later according to your taste buds
- Few shakes of pepper and a shake or two of Cayenne if you have it and like it
- 1 teaspoon each: garlic powder, dill weed, dried or fresh parsley, paprika
- Lemon juice of $\frac{1}{2}$ lemon, optional, gives it a little zing

59

If using thighs, put about a tablespoon of cooking oil in a large pot and sauté the thighs until both sides are slightly browned. If using leftovers, add then later on once all the vegetables are added.

Add onions and peppers, cook for a couple of minutes then add the carrots and celery and add 10 cups of water or broth.

Once the water is boiling for about 5 minutes, add the rest of the vegetables and all of the spices and lemon juice. Simmer for about 20 or 25 minutes. Add more broth or water if necessary, to cover all of the vegetables.

Pluck out one of each vegetable to make sure each variety is cooked. Adjust salt, pepper and garlic powder as needed.

CHAPTER NINE

*T*uesday morning. D-day. Day of the move. I was up early and wired on coffee, waiting for my folks to arrive. To kill time, I changed the bandages on my legs, designed a flier for the bistro's Valentine's Day special, then cleaned the floors, changed the cat litter and dusted. With the time dragging, I texted Matt, who was at work like everyone else I knew. That was the only drawback to not having the same day off as others. It got a bit lonely at times but usually I enjoyed the peace and solitude of my own company.

I checked in with Nicole as well to see if everything was okay. Her work schedule as a dance instructor was also jam packed during the early part of the week, so it was an hour before I heard back from her. A brief text just to say no strange calls, but Officer Sean was pursuing her relentlessly despite her telling him repeatedly to take a hike. He'd even shown up at her work with a cup of Tim Horton's coffee and a doughnut for her. It would have been sacrilegious to refuse such a gift, and I could hardly fault her for the moment of weakness.

I hadn't seen Nora for long on the previous day. She had dashed home, given Chicha more soup, changed clothes, and then ran right back out to meet (ugh) Leonardo. By the time she'd returned, I was already in bed.

61

The old bird was probably further with him than I was with Matt.

Shortly after ten in the morning, my parents arrived and came up for their key. Stephen had continued on to the house with the moving van. I grabbed the keys to my car and breathed a sigh of relief when I saw that the cops had removed the crime scene tape from my garage area during their visit the day before. I had no clue how I'd explain all this to my parents, and now I was given more time to come up with something brilliant.

My brother was stretching as we arrived. I walked over to him, punched him in the arm and told him he was fat and that his goatee made him look like a pimp. He complimented me sweetly on my mustache and told me I was getting a big Hungarian ass. This summed up our relationship beautifully. Note: I have neither a mustache nor a big ass...as of yet.

My parents loved the flowers as well as the new bottle of ice wine I had left for them. I had enjoyed it immensely so I knew they too would savor it. To my surprise, my mother cracked it open right away and took a swig straight from the bottle as I watched, partly in shock and partly in admiration. It was still morning! She smiled, and then announced she was ready to start moving in.

With his bad knee, my father moved slowly and handled the smaller things while the rest of us took care of everything else. I tried my best to conceal my wincing and limping, but to no avail. My mom stopped me with a big beefy hand on my shoulder and demanded to know what was wrong.

I showed her my injuries, peeling back one of the bandages, and explained what had happened. With her lips pressed firmly together, she poured me a glass from her bottle and told me to drink up. I shrugged and complied then we set back to work.

My mother is a small but stocky woman, with big, strong hands and equal determination. I had to struggle to keep pace with her, and by midafternoon the van was unpacked and most things were put away.

My brother ordered a pizza from Leonardo's and I made sure to stay out of sight, not knowing who would deliver. We were all too tired to make the one-minute drive to pick up the food. Then it struck me. Finally, I'd be able to order from Leonardo's, as long as he never found out that it was me calling from my parents' place. Maybe this move might turn out okay after all.

"So, how is bistro doing?" For some reason, my dad was speaking English.

"It's good, Dad. Of course, you were only gone a few days, so nothing's changed since you were last here," I lied shamelessly. This just wasn't the right time to bring up the most recent murder, and I didn't want to taint their first day at the new house anyway.

"You taking that accounting class yet?" Again in English.

"No, I'm too busy. And again, you've only been gone a few days!" My father had an obsession with me becoming an accountant despite the fact that I hated working with numbers and was not mathematically inclined. In fact, I barely passed the subject in high school.

"You still vut Mutt?"

"Yes, Mom, I'm still vut Mutt. Not much changes in just a few days. Nothing's changed." Well, if you didn't count the murder, nothing's changed. A half-truth.

We ate and then Stephen came over to my place for a while so that my parents could settle in without having us kids underfoot. Tempers were starting to flare so it was for the best. We slithered out while my parents were in the middle of a shouting match.

Back home, I fixed us a glass of my favorite non-wine drink, a Black Raspberry, my own creation. Raspberry vodka on ice topped with diet Pepsi. Whenever I was with my brother, I tended to reach for the mixed drinks instead of wine. I needed the hard liquor to tolerate him. In this case, I also needed it to numb the pain in my legs.

We had just sat back to relax when Nora bustled in with a grin on her face and carrying a bunch of Victoria's Secret bags. I introduced my brother and she joined us for a drink, smacking her lips in appreciation. "Boy, that's good stuff," she said, downing her glass and holding it out for a refill. "More please!"

"That reminds me, Steph, would you like to meet Nora's pig?" He looked confused.

"Do you mean her husband?" he asked, and Nora and I both laughed.

"No, I mean her pig. It's out in the back yard. Nora and her husband have recently split up, so Nora's staying here for a little while, with the pig."

"Okay, sure. I always like to get a good look at my breakfast," he joked and winked at Nora.

"By the way, Nora, I'll move Chicha back into the garage for you." Since the crime scene tape was gone, we could now use the garage again.

As we walked past her bags that rested on the floor by the entrance way, I caught a peek at a silky bra that looked similar to one I had recently bought. Now keep in mind, Nora is an older lady with several kids and even more grandkids. I did not want to know if she had gotten the matching thong, like I had. I looked over at her in surprise and she grinned her Cheshire cat grin, downing her second Black Raspberry in the blink of an eye and patting her stomach in a yum-yum gesture.

Stephen and I trudged out back to where the pig was lying inside the tent. I peered inside first and shrieked in surprise, backing away from the tent, getting it caught in my hair, falling, and almost taking it down with me. I peed a little. "What the hell are you doing here?!" I exclaimed.

"Relax, lady. It was snowing, and I noticed this tent, so I thought I'd get out of the snow for a while. The pig didn't seem to mind. Good soup, by the way."

Oh, my grossness! It was that guy on the blankets who

had taken my sandwich. And he'd eaten Chicha's soup! "Dude, this is getting weird. Who are you? Where do you live? And why are you eating the pig's food?"

"My name is Billy. I live *here* now," he said, spreading his arms in an arc.

"No, no, no you don't! You can't live here. *I* live here. And *the pig* lives here. You can't live with a pig. And you can't live with me. Do you need help? Is there someone I can call?" I shot my brother a look, warning him to stay calm. He could be inflammatory at the best of times, and I certainly didn't want to set this odd stranger off.

"Nah, I don't stay in touch with my family. But I need to buy some medicine. A little money would be nice, and I could use some more soup," he replied hopefully. I assumed that by medicine he meant drugs or alcohol, but he didn't elaborate and I did not pry.

"I'll bring you more soup, but you can't keep hanging around here. You know what, I shouldn't say this, but the house where you were the other day is empty right now. You can stay in that yard and it won't bother anyone. I'm sorry, you can't go inside, but you can take this tent with you if you'd like." Since we didn't need it anymore, and I didn't have much storage space, it seemed like a win-win situation. I made a mental note to tell Matt and to suggest that maybe he could go check on things at Joey's house and possibly persuade this guy to get some help.

"Thanks, lady, my very own place!" I wasn't sure if he was being sarcastic, but he looked happy even if a little nervous.

Stephen and I went back to the bistro, heated some soup for both Chicha and for Billy, and I found a to-go tin. A stab of Roman Catholic/Hungarian upbringing guilt made me also make a few sandwiches, and I packed them inside a bag with other odds and ends. Then I went upstairs and found an old black scarf, a matching hat and an old sweater that used to belong to Hans, my ex, which I was saving for cleaning toilets one day or wiping up vomit.

Leaving Stephen to chat with Nora, I went back outside and gave Billy the care package, telling him he could eat here but then he would have to leave. Despite my guilt, I was realistic enough to know that it was possible that he was dangerous, and that he wasn't my problem to fix. I am normally a compassionate person, and I strongly believe in karma and do my best to be nice to others. This, however, wasn't a stray kitten, and I had no intentions of keeping him.

I bribed Chicha into following me to the garage by again feeding her Cheerios. Returning upstairs, I caught the tail end of Nora and Steph's' conversation. "...you could stay here if you like. I'll be sleeping over at my boyfriend's house tonight. I'll change the spare bed for you." I gagged again, hearing Nora calling Leonardo her boyfriend and felt a twinge of sadness for her husband. I knew Craig and had no doubt that he was pretty torn up over the separation and would be even more torn up if he knew that Nora had a boyfriend.

As I entered the living room, I caught a fleeting glimpse of her and my mouth fell open. I was mistaken. She had changed and the new bra she was wearing was definitely nothing like the one I had purchased. My boobs certainly didn't rise up as high as her gals did! Stephen caught my eye and smirked.

"Interesting lady," he commented as she disappeared into her room. I just shrugged. I was speechless. We continued with our drinks in shocked silence until Nora rejoined us.

"I was able to get more information for you at the local stores, Mali," she began, slurping another drink. I widened my eyes to signal my panic but she took it as a look of encouragement. Before I could interrupt, she babbled on. "Turns out Alphie's girlfriend worked with him at the post office. I went to talk to her, but she was off yesterday."

"Thanks, Nora. I can actually go there myself; they don't know me yet so they won't know my history with

Leonardo. I just won't tell them my real name. Shouldn't you be going?" I changed the topic abruptly, hoping she'd take the hint.

"Oh, no, I have a few more minutes to visit and to have a little drink. Have you found out anything else about the murder?" She turned to Stephen, "Isn't it terrible that we had another murder here?"

Bless her inebriated little soul!

I slowly lifted my gaze to meet that of my brother. He sat patiently, smirking, one brow raised. I knew what he was thinking. Wait until Mom and Dad find out about this.

"I found a body in my garage. It has nothing to do with me." That summed it up and he didn't deserve an explanation anyway. I turned my attention back to Nora. "I found out that he lived in the subdivision where my parents just moved, and his wife is still there. I'm going to try to find out which house tomorrow when I deliver some fliers in the area, and I'll also zip by the post office."

"I see you're not getting involved this time," Stephen commented sarcastically.

"I'm not, really. Nora's done all the work so far." Nora beamed and sat up straighter as she swelled with pride. Her gals also swelled, if that was possible. Good grief, she'd have to be careful with those things!

"I guess I'll get going now," she said. Sure, why not? The damage was done.

"Do Mom and Dad know?" Stephen asked the obvious as soon as the door closed behind her.

"Not yet. I was hoping it would be all wrapped up before they moved, but they're here two weeks early. So, are you going to spend the night here?"

"Yeah, let's go over to their house and let them know that I'll stay here tonight and see if they need a last-minute hand with anything. Maybe they've stopped fighting by now."

My parents' phone wasn't connected yet, and they did not own a cell phone. Nor a computer, a tablet, nor anything else one might call modern. They still played movies on an old VCR that was the size of a microwave. And speaking of microwaves, they didn't own one of those, either. Mind you, the old VCR tended to get so overheated that it could likely have doubled as a microwave (I was pretty sure I could make a grilled cheese sandwich on top of it if hard pressed for a grill).

The visit lasted only minutes, and thankfully my brother didn't mention the murder, although he did toy with me a number of times, making me think he was about to spill the beans. Of course, they were happy Stephen would be staying at my place since they were exhausted and cranky and would soon be going to bed. This way, they wouldn't feel obligated to entertain him (with their VCR, no doubt, unless Lawrence Welk was on the tube again). Stephen drove the van over to my house and we were just settling back on the couch with fresh drinks when the bell rang.

Matt. Normally, I'd be thrilled, but my brother and he had not yet met. I had been hoping to put this day off for...well, forever. Stephen loved to tease me mercilessly, and if he could embarrass me in the process, it was a bonus. I wasn't looking forward to this. I downed the rest of my drink then answered the door.

Matt stepped inside and swooped me up in his arms, giving me a long passionate kiss before I could even say hello. He had me backed against the wall and was pressing against me, the heat building between us. The smell of his cologne filled my nostrils and made my mind swirl with pleasure. I could feel how happy he was to see me, and my body responded, pulling him closer.

"Are you trying to swallow her, buddy?" my brother asked. Matt leaped away as though I'd lit him on fire.

"Sorry," he stammered. "I didn't realize you had company. I just thought I'd stop by." He shot me a questioning glance. I hadn't had a chance to text or call him yet.

"Come on in, Matt, and meet my vile brother Stephen. He was helping my parents move in today." They shook hands and my brother smiled.

"I can see that you don't mind my sister's mustache," he stated pleasantly.

I slapped him on the head. "I do *not* have a mustache! You're such a pain in the ass. Grow up already!"

He snickered. "That's because you shaved it off."

I interrupted before he said anything else ridiculous. "Matt, before I forget, there's been a strange guy hanging around. I think he's homeless, and probably harmless, but we found him in the tent with Chicha today. I just wanted to get rid of him, so I suggested that he sleep in the back yard at Joey's house, and I gave him the tent that Sean gave to me. I was wondering if you could maybe swing by there and make sure he didn't break in, and maybe see if you can convince him to get help or something."

He frowned. "When did you first see this guy?"

"A few days ago, just after my new door was installed," I replied. "I gave him a sandwich." I thought it best not to mention that he'd actually demanded cash when he had burst through the door uninvited.

He frowned again. "So, just before Alphie was murdered?" He left the question hanging in the air until the implication dawned on me.

"Are you saying that this guy might somehow be involved?"

"Well, you say he's been hanging around. If he's not involved, then maybe he saw something. What do you say we head over there tomorrow for a chat? It's already dark, and frankly, I think I'd prefer to go during daylight."

We agreed that he'd come by after lunch the next day to pick me up, and then he was gone. If luck was on our side, maybe we'd even get a little time alone, with Nora still at work and with my brother gone. I'd have to remember to wear some cute under wear, although the injuries scabbing over on my legs were less than sexy.

CHAPTER TEN

I was too excited to sleep the next morning, and that pissed me off. I treasured my mornings and I'd been up early the previous day. I downed a couple of cups of coffee, had a quick breakfast of toasted rye bread slathered in crumbly garlic and herb goat cheese and then called Nicole. "What's your schedule today?" Wired from the caffeine, I got right to the point.

"I don't know; I'm still asleep. Beep. Please leave a message. What the heck's wrong with you, calling me at such a horrific hour? It's nine in the morning," she whined. "Let me think. We're Wednesday? I only have to be at the dance studio for one o'clock. Why?"

"I was wondering if you'd go to the post office with me. Apparently, Alphie's girlfriend worked there with him, and I wondered if you might recognize her. You'd mentioned something about two couples acting weird the night of the murder."

"I see where you're going with this," she said while yawning. "If it's her, then she was one of the last people to be with him, and she'd probably know who the other couple was. Just give me an hour and I'll be there."

71

The hour passed quickly. My brother had awakened, had a bite to eat then left to drive the moving van back to Montreal. I had just enough time to print three hundred copies of my Valentine's Day flier and to dust and sweep the bistro before Nicole arrived. We drove the short distance to the post office, which was almost right next to Leonardo's pizzeria.

As soon as we walked inside, Nicole started nodding like a bobble head doll. It was her. She was definitely the kind you'd remember with her platinum blonde hair, eyes thick with eyeliner and goopy mascara that clumped together in her lashes. The rest of her was pretty average looking.

I smiled brightly and asked for five stamps. I didn't need them but was bound to use at least five during the rest of the year. While she was counting them out, I said casually to Nicole, as though we'd been in the middle of a conversation; "...you're right, though; it sure is strange that his body was dumped at the bistro. Do you think it was a love triangle?"

The girl dropped the money I was handing her and the coins bounced everywhere. As we all helped to pick them up, I asked kindly, "Are you okay? You seem a little shaken."

"I'm so sorry." She fumbled with my change.

"Did you know the person who was killed? I didn't mean to be insensitive." I put on my best empathy voice.

"Yes. He was a co-worker...and a friend," she stammered as her eyes welled with tears before she quickly turned around, busying herself with a stack of envelopes.

"Please forgive me. I really am sorry."

She nodded curtly.

"You look familiar," Nicole spoke up. "I work at the Whine and Cheese bistro; I think I've seen you before. I'm sure I have." The girl's eyes flew to Nicole in a panic as she shook her head. "Yes, I remember you now. You were there last Friday. I remember admiring the shade of your blonde hair and wondering how it would look on me." I knew she was lying because she hated platinum. She amped up the charm and smiled sweetly. "That was *him* that you were with that night, isn't it?" The girl and I both gasped at her boldness.

"Shhhh," she hissed. "Please, my boss doesn't know. Yes, we were there, but when I last saw him, he was very much alive. I don't see how this is any of your business but I suggest you leave now."

I looked her squarely in the eye and lied, "My boyfriend works with the police. Would you prefer to speak with them instead?" Frankly, I was surprised they hadn't tracked her down yet. She shrank back in a panic. "Look, Nancy," I continued, reading her name tag, "I'm sure there are other people who were there that recognized at least one of you, so it's really just a matter of time until the cops come to speak with you. You might want to practice your story on us. If you guys were sneaking around, why go someplace so public?"

I could see her gulp before answering: "It's my fault. It was our anniversary. We'd been together for a year, and I wanted to go someplace nice. We figured we could act like we were just two co-workers out for a bite to eat and no one would be suspicious. It would have worked, too, if *they* hadn't walked in."Her eyes changed from teary to having a glint in them.

"They?" I prompted.

"Yeah. My ex-husband. With Alphie's wife." The glint in her eyes now shone fiercely.

"Were they...?" I didn't want to ask and I didn't have to.

"I'm sure they were," she snapped. "They walked in, sat down, and as soon as they saw us, they walked out again. They wouldn't have done that if they didn't have something to hide."

"I remember now. You ran out after them, didn't you?" Nicole interjected.

"Listen, Alphie just wanted to talk to them. After all, he

is...was...still married to her. Trust me, though, neither of them cared much about the marriage. Anyway, by the time we got out there they were already leaving the parking lot. We'd already paid for dinner and were just finishing our coffee at the time, so there was no point going back inside, so we left. He dropped me off at home and didn't bother staying since the mood was ruined anyway, if you get my meaning."

"What about your ex-husband? Have you heard from him?" I asked.

"Bob? Not a word, which I find strange. I thought he surely would have called, but no, not a single call or text. I guess I shouldn't be surprised; it wasn't an amicable divorce, let's just say."

I wasn't sure if it was my imagination, but she almost sounded disappointed, like she wanted him to call.

"Is there anything else, Nancy? Any guesses who might want Alphie dead?"

She snorted. "Half the town, including his wife, whom everyone seems to think is so sweet. But she has every bit of his anger...their Irish tempers raged when they were together."

"But I thought he was Leonardo's nephew," I said, confused. "Actually, now that I think about it, I thought Valerie was his favorite niece. I'm confused. Leonardo *is* Italian, isn't he?"

"Alphie was his nephew, but only by marriage since he was married to Valerie."

"But Leonardo *is* Italian, isn't he?" I repeated again. This still wasn't making sense.

She nodded. "Half. The other half is Irish. His real name is actually Lee, but he moved to Italy when he was still a young boy and grew up there. Of course they called him Leonardo, so he kept the name."

Half Irish and half Italian! Both nationalities known for having volatile tempers... Lucky me, to be on the receiving end.

We thanked her for speaking to us and offered our condolences once more. "Remind me again, why am I telling you all this?" she asked, confusion setting in again.

"Because we work there and want to clear up this mystery," I replied simply, failing to mention that I was the owner.

As we made our way back to the car, we noticed two officers heading into the post office. They'd finally tracked down the same lead we'd stumbled upon. I smiled proudly. We'd gotten there first. Had we gotten there later, Nancy would likely not have spoken to us, if she'd even stuck around.

"What we have to do now is track down her ex and Valerie," I said, regretting that I hadn't thought to ask Nancy which house Valerie lived in and where Bob worked and lived.

"And you'll have to do that on your own, because I have to head off to work soon. How about feeding me first?" She grinned, licking her lips in anticipation.

"I suppose it's the least I can do. Brilliant move on your part, by the way, breaking Nancy down so quickly and piecing things together." Nicole grinned, looking very proud.

We returned to the bistro and I cut bits of my all-time favorite bread, sour dough, slathered them with pâté and then on the side some thinly-sliced, hot Hungarian salami. We ate our open-faced sandwiches in peace while I doodled on a note pad.

Without realizing it, I had drawn Alphie's name in the middle and drawn little branches extending out to Valerie, Bob, Nancy and Leonardo's names and then beyond that, a multitude of branches but with no names.

"What are the no-name ones?" Nicole asked, peering at my doodles.

"So far, half the town apparently hates him. Oh, and one branch for the ski-doers—they hated him too."

"That's a lot of people already. But do you really think

Nancy would want him dead ?"

"I don't know," I replied. "He did run out of the bistro after his wife. That might have ticked her off, since it was their anniversary, after all, and it was supposed to be their special day." She nodded in agreement.

We finished eating and she hurried off to work, moaning something about having to dance with a full belly. Since her stomach was perfectly flat and enviably muscular, I wasn't particularly sympathetic.

I admired my scabs for a while and decided not to re-bandage them. They were healing well and although my legs still ached, I could now walk without much of a limp. With that thought in mind, I set out for my next task.

I gathered the fliers that I had printed earlier and headed to my parent's subdivision. Leaving their house for last, I busied myself with the task at hand. In this area, no one had mailboxes, as everyone got their mail from their designated mail slot located at the corner of each street. As mail could only be accessed via a key, I had no choice but to go to each house, which worked into my plans perfectly as my main goal on this day was to try to track down Valerie.

I had taped one to the communal mailbox, then set about going door to door, giving people the fliers if they answered the door or leaving them on the porch if they didn't. I made small talk, introduced myself and told them I hoped to see them at the bistro soon. Small talk with strangers was never something in which I particularly excelled, very likely as a result of having been severely shy in my youth. I took comfort in the knowledge that there were only a few houses left to visit.

Near the end of the third and last street in the subdivision, Gopher Crescent, I hit the jackpot.

A lady with bleary, red-rimmed eyes answered the door, looking at me suspiciously. Her dark hair was pulled back into a ponytail and she wore rumpled sweat pants and a t-shirt that had what looked like chocolate stains on it. "Go away," she snapped rather viciously. "I'm done talking with reporters. Why don't you all just leave me alone?" Apparently she had mistaken the fliers I was holding for a pad of paper.

"I'm not a reporter. I'm the owner of the Whine and Cheese bistro, and I just wanted to give you this flier so you'd know about our Valentine's Day special. I'm so sorry, I didn't realize whose house this was, but you're Valerie Brut, aren't you?"

She looked closely at me. "Do I know you?" she asked.

"No, but we have a mutual friend. Please accept my condolences; this must be a very hard time for you." She nodded and took the flier from me, to my relief not bothering to ask who our mutual friend might be.

"I realize you might not want to come to the bistro, since your uncle hates me for some reason and...well... with Mr. Brut being found there. But I would like to invite you as my personal guest, free of charge, whenever you feel you're ready to venture out."

"Uncle Leo wouldn't like that very much. He'd say I'm eating with the enemy," she said with a tremulous little smile.

"Yes, but you were already there recently, were you not? I do hope you come back again," I stated simply and watched her blanch.

"If you will excuse me..." she said huffily. But I interrupted.

"Yes, that night, the night of the *incident*." I faltered then blundered on quickly. "I had heard that you were there with a fellow named Bob, but that you hadn't stayed long." She glared at me and slammed the door in my face. Not quite sure what to do next, I rang the bell again, but not surprisingly, she refused to answer. I grinned to myself, considering this a victory and concluding that she wouldn't be so touchy if she weren't trying to hide something.

I delivered the rest of the fliers then popped in to

check on the Aliens. I noted with horror that they'd wasted no time hanging my mom's framed, cross-stitched pictures that she'd sewn by hand over the past two decades. They must have had a good forty of those dust traps hanging on the walls. My mom beamed with pride when she caught me looking at them. "These will all be yours and Stephen's one day," she stated, misinterpreting my look to be one of envy.

"Oh, Mom, you know I would love that, but Steph will be the lucky one. My allergies just couldn't handle it," I said, barely able to keep the dismay out of my voice. There was no way that those atrocities would ever be on my walls, allergies or not! "Anyway, let me look around and see what you guys have done," I changed the subject quickly.

They had worked tirelessly until pretty much everything was in place.

"Why don't you two join me for dinner tonight?" I suggested, noting the dark circles under my mother's eyes and my dad's exhausted expression. "You must be tired from the move and all the unpacking?" I figured I owed it to them to be a good daughter and at least cook dinner for them. The Whine would be open the next few nights, so I wouldn't be seeing them again for a few days. They agreed to come over later and I arrived back at my house just as Matt was arriving for our outing to go find Billy.

CHAPTER ELEVEN

"Come in for a minute, Matt, so I can store these away." We went in through the back door and I put the remaining fliers in my office. "How about a coffee before we head back out?" I called. "I haven't had one in hours and I could use a little pick-me-up!" Socializing had drained me to my core, which also reminded me to take my early afternoon thyroid pill.

Matt prepared the coffee while I made a couple of ham and cheese sandwiches to take to Billy. As I was preparing them, Matt came up behind me, slipped his arms around my waist and nuzzled my neck. "I can't wait to get you alone," he whispered in my ear and reached one hand up towards my face but accidentally grazed a breast in the process. Surprised, I nipped my finger with the knife I had in my hand and yelped.

"Well, you can have me alone, but first you'll have to endure a dinner with my parents tonight. Will you join us? They won't stay late. Nora's still here, too, but I'm fairly certain that she'll be going to Leonardo's since she slept there last night."

Matt raised an eyebrow to that. "The sly ol' dog," he

muttered, clearly impressed. "The Granny scored?" I think he was jealous. I know I was.

He wrapped a Band-Aid around my bleeding finger and then kissed the tip gently. He glanced up and caught my gaze, then kissed my palm. His lips continued their journey up to the inside of my elbow then slowly up to my shoulder. Losing all restraint, I grabbed his longish hair and pulled him closer for a deep kiss, and our tongues intertwined. Without any recollection of how it happened, his shirt and mine found their way to the floor.

In one swift movement, he propped me up on the counter next to the sandwiches and again I pulled him close, wrapping my legs around him and tired of my inner turmoil about how long I should wait before sleeping with him.

His mouth trailed back down my neck and to my chest before I realized my bottom was warm and wet. I worried suddenly that I may have lost control of my bladder in my excitement. Through bleary half closed eyes, I looked down at the counter and groaned. He mistook it for a groan of pleasure as his tongue flicked against my skin.

"Matt, the coffee!"

"Not right now," he muttered, flicking his tongue just barely inside my bra. I gasped at the sensation.

"No," I said with a shaky voice, "the coffee is all over the counter. I'm sitting in it!"

That got his attention and we both laughed. He'd forgotten to put the coffee pot in place before pressing the start button!

"I guess it's just not meant to happen yet, Matt," I said, the sensual fog now dissipating. "We have to check on Billy, anyway." We quickly dressed and cleaned up the counter. Luckily, I had already wrapped the sandwiches in plastic so they were spared.

Matt sat on one of the couches in the bistro while I went up to change out of my wet jeans. I made him wait downstairs since I couldn't trust myself to be alone with him and didn't want our first time to be rushed, especially when I knew my parents and Nora would arrive soon. And it would be just like Nora to pop up when we least expected it.

Wearing fresh clothes, I made my way through the bistro to where Matt was waiting. The Whine is furnished with reds, blacks and grays and has some couches, club chairs, high, glossy round tables with stools and a piano area where Nicole, who is multi-talented, sometimes sings jazzy songs.

There's also a bar area that has a glass display cabinet next to it, which showcases my quirky bottles of wine and other various wine gadgets, such as glasses, coasters, wine stoppers, anything and everything I could get my hands on that had to do with wine—all for sale, of course, and always with a theme.

The current theme was Valentine's Day and featured big red wine glasses and bottles of Passion, Frisky Zebras, Naked Rebel and Saint Amour. The display wasn't finished yet and I reminded myself that I still had to get my hands on some bottles of Fifty Shades of Grey (that naughty trilogy now came in a liquid format).

I walked over to the couch where Matt was stretched out with his eyes closed. His looks still always took me by surprise and made my breath hitch. Sometimes, when I drank a bit too much, it was hard not to call him Keith due to his similarities to Keith Urban. Again unable to resist, I straddled him with my legs and brought my lips to his.

I could feel him smile as he wrapped me in his arms, sighing. "We either leave now, or we take our clothes off right here," he threatened. I gave him one last quick kiss, and then toyed with my top button seductively before launching off so quickly that I turned my ankle slightly and stumbled. The mood broken, he shook his head slightly, laughing softly at my expense while I hobbled towards the back door. At least now if I limped, he'd think it was because of the ankle and I wouldn't have to tell him about the embarrassing grocery cart incident.

We drove to Joey's house, holding hands and grinning like teenagers. Upon arrival, we noted that neither Billy, nor the tent, were anywhere to be seen. To my surprise, Matt walked up to the front door and unlocked it with a key. Seeing my confusion, he shrugged sadly and explained.

"His will was read the other day." He paused for composure. "He left the house to me, but I'm not sure what I'm going to do with it." He sighed, looking around him. Joey, as his parents before him, had been a hoarder, and although some feeble attempts had been made at getting rid of some things, there was still very little room to move about inside. I was thankful, however, that despite the chaos, everything was relatively clean. I had been in here once before, but only briefly, and at the time didn't have much of a chance to look around. It shocked me that people could live like this.

Maybe it was a residual effect from my childhood and the plethora of framed cross-stitches, but I myself had never been much of a fan of having unnecessary items in my life. Other than some decorative candles and the odd painting, I didn't have extra furniture or knick-knacks in my house, and I quickly started to feel claustrophobic and, irrationally, dirty. We searched the inside of the house quickly, in case Billy had somehow gotten in, but he was nowhere to be found.

"Why don't we check the trails? Matt suggested. I readily agreed, wanting to escape from the house as quickly as possible.

We got about a half mile into the trail before we heard a voice. "Hey, lady! Is that a bag of food?" We looked around and finally spotted him about a hundred feet off the trail. He had set up the tent and was sitting by the opening. He waved half-heartedly, almost as though lifting his hand took all his strength.

We made our way to where he was camped and I gave

him the sandwiches. He took them cautiously, and then hungrily tore into one, mumbling his thanks. I introduced him to Matt and he nodded. "I've seen you there," he mumbled. My hackles rose.

"What do you mean, you've seen him there? When, Billy?" I asked cautiously. Had he been spying on me?

"I've been around for a couple of weeks now. I see things. I can't always remember them too good though." He shrugged. "I've seen him and your blonde friend and the one with the dark curly hair a lot. I like her," he whispered wistfully. He was referring to Chloé.

"Have you been watching my place?" I asked.

"I've been in and out of the trails. I notice things. Sometimes you would leave your garage door unlocked, so I slept in there a couple of times until that pig showed up and they did something to that guy there. I think they were after me, but I outsmarted them." His voice grew quiet again and then he laughed oddly. Suddenly looking uneasy, he glanced around then cocked his head to one side. Without another word, he bolted further into the forest, leaving everything behind. He was out of sight within seconds.

"That was bizarre," Matt said.

"Did you hear what he said? He said something about the guy in my garage. Do you think he actually did get killed there? And that he saw it?"

"I think I'd like to talk to him again. It sounds to me like he might have seen something," Matt stated. "Let's come back again after dinner to see if he returns. Maybe we can get a bit more information out of him."

I nervously agreed. I wasn't too keen on returning in the dark, but I was curious for more information. I was also convinced that the police knew nothing of Billy, so it was clear to me that we now had the lead on the murder investigation.

"Of course, who's to say he's not the killer?" I said to Matt.

He shook his head in disagreement. "No. He seems a bit off, but I don't think he's a killer. You were right when you suggested that he needs help." He threw twenty bucks into Billy's tent, looking around quickly. The only thing inside other than the blankets and what I had given him was a ratty backpack. Matt hesitated, then quickly unzipped the pockets on the bag and rummaged through it.

"No I.D.—nothing. Just a change of clothes..." He shook his head sadly. "The guy definitely needs help."

We trekked back to Matt's car and returned to the bistro in silence, our earlier romantic mood forgotten. Back at the house, Matt helped me whip up a batch of Nora's soup, but this time I added some homemade Hungarian egg noodles and some sour cream instead of the lemon juice. I had grown up eating homemade soup at least once a week, so I knew this was a safe bet with my parents.

By the time they arrived, the table was set, a loaf of fluffy white Italian bread was warming in the oven and some wine was chilling.

"Mutt, hallo, you heer too?" My dad said.

"Yes, Mr. Kis, I'm here too. Nice to see you again." He shook hands with my dad and kissed my mom on both cheeks, European style. A moment later, Nora bustled in, shaking snow from her hair.

"I can't believe it's snowing again!" she exclaimed. "I don't think winter is ever going to end in this city!" She took off her coat and I saw my dad's eyes bug out. Oh no!

"Nora! You went to work like that?" I gasped before I could stop myself.

"What's wrong with what I have on?" she asked defensively.

"Well, there's nothing...wrong with it, I guess. But...the bra! Isn't it a bit perky for work?" I suggested as delicately as I could, trying to remove my proverbial foot from my mouth.

84

"Oh, that... Yeah, I know. I forgot to bring a change of clothes with me to Leo's last night and I didn't want to wake you early this morning by coming home. My boss did casually remind me that we have a dress code at work." She blushed, and then smiled at my folks.

I made the introductions and my dad fought to hide his grin. Although there's no end to the negative things I can say about him, I do have to admit that he is a joker by nature, and I hoped he'd have it in him to hold his tongue. As Nora went off to her room to change, he finally got it out of his system. "Son ovva gun!" he exclaimed. "Mama, ve gonna getting you something like dat!"

My mother laughed nervously and blushed.

I knocked on Nora's door. "Will you be joining us for dinner, Nora?"

"Yeah, I'll join you in a moment. I'll be staying in tonight. I tell you, I'm positively bushed. Leo kept me up all night!" I grimaced at the thought, but had to admit I was envious. I'd love to have that chance myself, but with Matt, of course. On a good note, I noticed that my gag reflex wasn't immediately activated anymore when she spoke of Leo.

I carved up a creamy wedge of Oka cheese, one of my dad's favorites, and added Irish Cheddar and some light marbled cheddar to the plate. We munched and enjoyed our wine, a bottle of Sexy rosé, while we waited for Nora. I savored the sweet, slightly strawberry-like flavor and sucked it back in record time, reaching for seconds.

When she joined us, we all discreetly glanced at her chest. Everything was back to normal, though I suspected that I detected a glimmer of disappointment in my dad's eyes.

"So, Mama has a soorprize for you," my dad announced as my mother leaped up to get her purse. She came back holding a piece of paper as my dad explained that they'd gone to the corner store earlier and saw some signs announcing classes at the local community center.And my mom apparently thought it would be fun if she and I took a class together. I groaned. No doubt it would be an accounting class.

"For the last time, Dad, I'm not interested in accounting classes," I said a bit more sharply than I intended. My mom snickered. "No accounting. You and I, ve gonna go dancing!" She hummed a crazy little tune and did a little jig. "La, la, la-la-la-la-lahhhhh...

What the heck?

"Ve do polish dancing. Da Polka!" My mom exclaimed, beaming. She handed me the paper with the class title, dates and times: Tuesday night; seven o'clock. But wait...

"Mom, did you for saying Polish dancing?" OMG, there it was! I was talking like them! I've long ago given up looking for an explanation. If I'm around them too long, I start speaking like them. Yes, I turn into an alien.

"Ya, Polish.Ve have fun!"

I started to laugh softly but was unable to contain it for long and it soon escalated out of control. After a minute, I had tears streaming down my face. Curious, Matt took the paper from my hands, read it quickly, and then grinned like a shark.

"Vat is vrong?" my dad asked. In between laughing and tears, I was finally able to get a few strangled words out.

"It's not Polish dancing; it's POLE dancing. Mom and I are going to learn to dance like strippers!" I was almost rolling on the floor at this point, holding onto my bladder to keep from peeing myself. And...yeah...what can I say, I peed a little.

"Oh boy!' my mom exclaimed. "No, I don't do that." She blushed furiously.

"Oh, yes you will! There's no way I'm going alone! We're in this together. Mother-daughter bonding," I said.

"I'll go if you don't want to, Mrs. Kis," Nora piped up. My dad and Matt grinned, no doubt picturing her with her push up bra. My mother quickly agreed, happy to be off the hook. Although she would have had fun doing a Polka,

I knew pole dancing would be out of her comfort zone. I would have paid to see it though.

"Thanks for the gift, Mom. Nora and I will go. It was very thoughtful of you. And we'll find something else to do together," I said to cheer her up. "Now then, let's have dinner."

The rest of the evening was quiet, other than the few times that I'd burst out laughing when I'd picture my mom pole dancing. There was also a tense moment when they critiqued my soup, commenting that I should have added some Hungarian sausage to it. They left shortly after dinner, and Nora also bid us good night, going to bed early.

Matt and I prepared for our outing into the trails, testing the flashlights to make sure the batteries still worked. I packed up the leftovers, muttering to myself about Hungarian sausage, and then we went to Joey's for the second time that day.

We headed into the forest and had walked to the point that we'd marked earlier with a pile of rocks, so that we'd remember where the tent had been. We set off to the right of the trail, but the tent was gone. We weren't about to wander around in the darkness for longer than we had to, so we headed back to Joey's house. I left the soup by the front door just in case Billy returned. I couldn't shake the feeling that we were being watched; he was out there, I could feel it, my gypsy senses tingled. Why was he hiding? Was he on the run? Or, was he stalking us and waiting for his chance to whack us? Was he the one that had killed Alphie?

The more I thought about it, the more nervous I became, until I was convinced we were about to die. Almost hysterical, I nearly ran to the car, urging Matt to hurry. He must have felt my vibes because he didn't dawdle.

We drove back to the house and Matt parked his car next to mine. As I got out, I stopped, looking at my car.

Something didn't seem right. I walked around it and my heart sank. I had one flat tire. But it wasn't just flat. It had been slashed, many times. "Crap!" I exclaimed.

Matt joined me, and as the ex-cop in him kicked in and he quickly scanned the area, his expression turned grim. "I hate to tell you this, Mali, but it looks like you're involved again. This appears to have turned personal. Who have you pissed off lately? I told you not to get involved."

Oh, he shouldn't have said that.

As though sensing the shift in my mood, he grabbed me and hugged me. "I just want you to be safe. I'm not going to tell you what to do. Hop back inside my car and we'll go get you a new tire, but we have to hurry if we want to get there before they close. Please," he added, to ensure that it didn't sound like an order. I huffed grudgingly but complied, slamming the car door to show my displeasure.

We were there and back within an hour, and Matt changed my tire while I held one of the flashlights to give him light. The other was on the ground in the snow. In the light, we could see footprints leading to and from my car, and we cautiously followed them. Surprisingly, they led to the main road and then disappeared.

"I wasn't expecting that," Matt said.

"What were you expecting?" I asked, almost afraid to hear his answer.

"I thought they'd lead to the trails. This, however, would indicate that someone parked on the road and walked into your parking lot from there. Let's take a precautionary look around your property and then go inside and try to make sense of it. Please," he added again for good measure. To be honest, 'please' was starting to piss me off.

We peered inside the garage and were greeted by Chicha's snort and squinting eyes when I turned on the light. Matt cautiously looked at the back of the garage, where Alphie had been found. All was clear. We exited then continued our search of the property. At the back of the house, Matt stopped suddenly and I stumbled right into him.

"What's wrong?" I whispered. I stepped out from behind him and gasped.

The tent!

We approached quietly, and at the opening I called out Billy's name. No answer. I said it a little louder. Again, there was no answer. I stood back and Matt opened the zipper, which was already half open, and took a look inside. The tent was empty. We heard rustling in the trails but the sound soon disappeared, unless we had both imagined it. "Do you think that was Billy?" My voice shook a little as I spoke.

Matt nodded. "More than likely. But since the tent is here, I don't think he's responsible for your slashed tire. That would be like pointing the finger directly at himself. Oddly, I get the sense that he feels safe here. That's interesting. Let's go inside".

"Shouldn't we call the cops?" I asked.

"If you feel like waiting for them to show up and then having them look around, as we just did, then having them ask questions about the tent and about Billy, then sure." He was right, it would be a waste of time and I didn't want Billy hauled away when he clearly needed help of a very different kind.

I poured us some of that deliciously sweet ice-wine. I was sad that just under half a bottle remained, and I savored each sip. My eyes were drawn to the label: Inniskillin... Ice Wine... Inniskillin... Certainly, my subconscious was trying to tell me something, but what was it? My aneurism twitched. Shaking my head, I pushed the niggling feeling aside for the moment and filled Matt in on all the details of what I'd unearthed so far.

"By the way," I said, "you never told me what happened when you followed the ski-do guy who was hitting on me that night." What the heck was his name? Biff? Brutus? Oh yes, Markus.

"That was quite informative, actually, though not very exciting. I'm not sure what to make of it yet, but there's something there. I can feel it. He was the first of that ski-do crowd to leave that night. I followed him, but all he did was park in front of a house near where your parents live. What was interesting, though, was that I wasn't the only one following him." Matt paused to remember then continued. "Another car was already behind him before me. Whoever it was had parked a few hundred feet away, and I parked at a cross street where I had a good view of them both. I couldn't make out the other driver though. He, or she, was wearing a baseball hat, but that's all I could see. If it was a guy, he wasn't tall, but it could just as easily have been a female. About an hour later, Markus drove away and the other car followed at a safe distance. From what I could tell, he went home after that. The other car drove right past the house where Markus appeared to live and then lost me on the highway at a red light."

"Did anything happen at the house that he was watching?" I asked.

"It was pitch black, so I don't know if whoever was there was asleep or just not home."

I sat, chewing at my lip. I was pretty sure the house belonged to Valerie, Alphie's wife. Why would Markus be watching her house? And who was watching him? His wife? Valerie's new boyfriend, Bob? That was Sunday night, but from what Nicole had said, the ski-do crowd had also been at the Whine on Friday night, the night Alphie was killed. Was Markus there at the same time that Alphie had been? And did he see Valerie with Bob, and Alphie with Nancy, that night? Was there another love triangle here? How many triangles were we dealing with? And why did they all come to my bistro? And if you put all the triangles together, did that make a rectangle? My head was spinning and a giggle rippled out of me as I realized I was becoming silly.

"I'm pretty sure that the house he was watching

90

belongs to Alphie's wife," I said to Matt. "There's definitely something going on there. We've got to get in with that ski-do crowd. The more I think about it, the more that's the key to all this."

"You're not going anywhere with that greasy Markus!" Matt exclaimed. "And this time it is an order. Please," he clarified, in case I had any doubt. I didn't take offence since I agreed whole-heartedly that he was greasy.

"Not me, silly! I was thinking of Chloé. She was getting pretty chummy with one of the guys Sunday night after I asked her to take over the table for me. She's pretty adventurous, you know. Maybe she can hang out with the crowd to see what she can find out." I grinned to myself for a moment, envisioning Chloé, wearing her signature killer heels while riding on the back of a ski-do.

My head was now pounding, and it was getting late. To my surprise, Matt asked for a spare blanket, announcing that he'd be sleeping on the couch. The tire slashing episode had him nervous and he didn't want to worry about me all night. I thought for a minute, and then took a plunge.

"How about you just sleep with me? We're grownups, right? Plus, Nora's way ahead of us with Mr. Leonardo, so I hardly think she'll have anything to say about you spending the night with me. I'm sure we can control ourselves." Okay, maybe I wasn't too sure, but suddenly my headache was starting to ease.

Matt ran his hands through his hair, then grabbed me swiftly and gave me a quick kiss before leaping up from the couch and distancing himself from me. "There's nothing I'd like more, but I have an early morning meeting tomorrow, and if I sleep with you, I won't actually get a wink of sleep, and you know it. It's best if I sleep on your couch...this time." His eyes smoldered.

I grinned, knowing I couldn't argue. If he were in my bed, the last thing I'd be doing is sleeping. I rustled up what I could for extra bedding, slim pickings after all the blankets that I'd given to Chicha and to Billy, but I managed. Finally, I had him settled on the couch, gave him a quick but gentle good night kiss and went off to my own bed.

CHAPTER TWELVE

Sure, I went off to my own bed, *eventually*. First, I had a hot and steamy shower to ease the last of the headache. It worked, but it also succeeded in arousing me further than the thought of Matt on my couch already had. I tossed and turned for a while in bed, finally picking up a book that I was in the middle of reading. With my luck, I just happened to be at the part where the main characters were in a steamy love scene. Frustrated, I finally peeked out my bedroom door and stood there, listening.

Not a sound. No one was stirring except Hummer, who looked up from his spot next to the couch, where he was watching Matt with a wary eye. I tiptoed over and stood next to him, hesitating. Now what? Jump him? I started giggling to myself at the thought and had to clamp a hand over my mouth and quickly tiptoe back to my room to the let out the laugh.

After regaining control, I tiptoed back out and again stood next to him, contemplating my next move.

"Are you going to just stand there all night or are you going to join me?" Matt asked in a husky voice. What could I say? I crawled in next to him, my body flush with

93

his on the narrow couch.

We lay like that for a few minutes before his lips found mine then traced a path to my neck. When he reached that spot just below my ear, I couldn't take it anymore. I reached for his zipper, lowering it carefully. His breath was ragged, as was mine. I was gently snaking my hand in through the opening and...Nora's blasted door opened. We froze, with my hand down his pants and his fingertips down my jammies.

We listened to her shuffle down the hall to the bathroom. Without a word, we both got to our feet and hurried to my room, closing the door and tumbling onto my bed. Impatiently, I reached for his waistband, struggling to tug his pants and boxers lower.

With one swift movement, he removed my PJ bottoms and the last of his clothes and we lay next to each other, skin against skin, our lips finding each other again, lips and hands exploring, not caring if the bed creaked or the floors shook. It had been a long two years of celibacy for me and I was only thankful that we didn't break the bed with our enthusiasm.

Needless to say, we got no sleep. Matt had to leave early and I walked him to the door, reluctant to part with him, his scent and presence tugging at me like a drug. After a last, tender, lingering kiss, he left just as Nora ambled out of her room. She stopped, squinted at the blanket on the couch before shifting her gaze to me and my rumpled hair. She looked at me shrewdly and nodded. "It's about time. It was like standing next to a volcano about to erupt whenever the two of you were in a room together." I grinned foolishly at the comparison but didn't bother to deny it.

"I'll see you at work tonight, and I already asked Chloé to take my shift on Friday so I can see Leo. She was hoping some ski-do guy would show up that she met recently. I hope she's not looking for trouble." She walked down the hall to the bathroom to get ready for work. It was only six in the morning so I crawled into bed and slept straight through until eleven.

Upon waking, I remembered the details of the night before and stretched deliciously, every nerve ending tingling with renewed energy and desire until I remembered my slashed tire. With that sobering thought, I launched out of bed. I had clues to hunt down and tonight was Thursday, which meant the Whine would be open at four o'clock in the afternoon. I dressed hastily, pleased to see that my wounded legs had survived the activities of the night before unscathed, and downed a quick cup of coffee. There would be no time for lounging in bed and watching the food channel today.

Hummer glared at me as I gathered the sheets and blanket from the couch. "Sorry, buddy. It was bound to happen. You'll grow to like Matt, I'm sure." I gave him a long hug and buried my nose in his tabby fur until he struggled to break free with a squawk.

Emboldened by my night of passion, the first thing I did was drive to the pizza place. Mr. Leonardo was right where I wanted him to be, at the front counter. I had no sooner walked inside than he glanced about wildly, looking for something to throw at me, and snarling, "You get out! Why do you keep coming here, foolish girl? Can't you see that I'm busy, eh?" I looked quickly and noticed that I was the only customer.

"Just listen for one minute," I spoke hurriedly. "Someone is following your niece, Valerie."

That got his attention and he lowered the jar of homemade garlic sauce with which he had armed himself.

"Who is following her?" His eyes narrowed as he gestured grudgingly for me to sit at one of the tables near the counter. I sat as he stood, still holding the garlic sauce.

"Why don't you put that thing down while we talk?" I asked hopefully. He shook his head and narrowed his eyes further.

"You look different today," he remarked, cocking his

head to one side. I blushed furiously and changed the subject.

I began hesitantly. "I'm not sure who was following Valerie," I lied, not wanting to give him more than what I'd get out of him, and also not wanting to drag Matt into this. "There was someone in my bistro the other night who was causing a scene. Later, I followed him, hoping to find out where he lived. Instead of going home though, he parked in front of Valerie's house for an hour, just watching. I don't know why someone would do that? Could your niece be in danger?"

His head shook like a bobble-toy. "Those two! Crazy, both of them! I love my niece but she's just as crazy as Alphonso. That's why we try to make sure she doesn't find out about him cheating."

"Are you saying that she was cheating on him, too?"

Anger flared in his eyes, and then quickly dissipated. He sighed deeply. "She was running around town with that Markus for a while. I told her to be careful, not to be with someone that Alphie ski-doed with. But she doesn't care what I think. Or what anybody else thinks. I think she likes the challenge of not getting caught."

That surprised me and I tried not to show any emotion. I had been expecting to have a conversation about Bob, who did not ski-do. If what Mr. Leonardo said was true, she had been seeing Markus. Was that why he'd lurked in front of her house for an hour? He must have seen her with Bob at the bistro that night. Things were starting to get complicated. To thank him for this information, I decided to give him a bit in return.

"It may have been Markus who was parked at her house. I do remember that name being mentioned at the bistro. A big guy with a beard?" I asked, playing it cool. He nodded. He still hadn't bashed me with garlic sauce. Things were looking up.

"Do you know when Valerie stopped seeing him?"

He studied me for a moment and glanced briefly at the

jar in his hand. I sat up straighter, ready to duck if necessary.

"Why do *you* want to know?" he asked.

I drew a deep breath and leveled with him. "Someone was either killed or dumped at my bistro...again, and then my tire was slashed yesterday. It would seem that everyone involved was at my bistro at some point, and I'm tired of people involving me in all this. I just want to pour wine and serve cheese and not have extra drama in my life, Mr. Leonardo."

I was greeted by silence. I studied him carefully, noting that his features were slowly growing rigid. He clutched the jar tighter and a vein popped up in his hand. Then he spoke softly, so softly that I had to strain to hear. "Valerie went to your bistro?" I nodded and then belatedly recalled the phrase she had used if he found out, eating with the enemy. *"Traditore!"* he swore under his breath.

"She a stopped seeing him about two months ago. She met someone else, I think. She looked happy and sneaky, like she was hiding a secret."

"Was Alphie already seeing Nancy at the post office by then?" I asked.

He nodded. "But not just her..." My eyes widened. The guy was cheating on his girlfriend *and* his wife?

"Do you think either of them knew?"

He shrugged. "He never cared who knew."

I asked the obvious: "Do you know who it was?"

"No. I saw him at the grocery store buying three bouquets of flowers. He told me he'd cut me off at the knees if I said anything."

"Do you think he really had connections that would do that, or was it an act? Or would he do that himself?"

Again he shrugged. "I don't know, and I don't want to find out." He looked sad, and I almost felt sorry for him.

Not knowing what else to ask, and figuring that I'd gotten what I could from him, I thanked him and asked if he'd like me to keep him informed. Almost imperceptibly, he nodded.

Once inside my car, I quickly jotted down some notes, not wanting to forget details. One side effect from having thyroid issues is an occasional memory lapse, and this was too important to chance that. My car was parked directly across from the post office, and as I paused from my writing for a moment, I watched Nancy milling about. Would my luck continue?

She glanced about wildly as I entered. "It's just me," I reassured her. "I wanted to make sure you're okay. I saw the cops come in the other day after I left. Did that go okay?"

She came out from behind the counter to speak to me. "My boss is working in back. I can't talk long. Yes, everything went okay. It actually wasn't too bad; you were right. Having had a chance to tell you my side of things made it easier when I had to speak to them."

She didn't seem to bear ill feelings toward me, and I smiled sympathetically. She seemed like a nice girl who had just gotten entangled with the wrong guy. I felt bad for what I was about to say next, until I saw a bandage on her right hand and my breath caught in my throat. "What happened to your hand?" I asked, holding my breath while I waited for the answer.

"Oh, it's nothing really. I was using one of those box cutting knives and it slipped. I'm pretty clumsy." She laughed at herself while I subconsciously took a step backward. Could she have been the one who slashed my tire? Or to stab something through Alphie's eye?

"Did you know that Alphie had another girlfriend?" I blurted. Maybe there was more to this wisp of a girl than I originally thought.

She laughed. "Sweetie, he had many; it's no surprise."

"No... I mean, at the same time as you?" She blanched and her lips quivered. I took that to mean that she hadn't known after all.

"Who?" she whispered.

"That I don't know, but it might be the key to this whole mystery."

She stood quietly, nodding her head. "That explains some things then. I only saw him once a week during the past couple of weeks, and at work, of course. He just said that Valerie was breathing down his neck about not being home, so he had to be a bit more careful. I should have known it wasn't true; he'd never cared what she thought before. Listen, I have to get back to work. Thanks again for letting me know." She cut the conversation off quickly and hurried to the back room of the post office. A moment later another lady, whom I assumed was her boss, emerged. "Hello, may I help you?"

I smiled, "Five stamps, please." Sigh, I'd now have to find ten reasons to mail something this year.

I slipped the stamps into my purse and returned home. It was time to start preparing the daily hot dish for the bistro so I had to hurry as I had spent more time investigating than I had anticipated. I brought Chicha a bowl of soup and some Cheerios and noted she wasn't sneezing anymore. I also noticed that the tent was gone.

I was up to my elbows in peeled potatoes and cooked lean ground beef when Nicole rushed in, slamming the door shut behind her and swearing in French under her breath. "*Merde!*" she exclaimed one last time as she threw her purse onto the floor.

"Everything okay?" I asked.

She looked at me curiously, her fury suddenly evaporating. First from the left, then from the right, circling me like a shark and then suddenly grinning from ear to ear, she said, "Well, it's about time!" She squealed and gave me a fierce hug. "Was it good?" she asked. "Of course it was good! It was, wasn't it?" She gushed as I blushed furiously and wiped my face on my sleeve.

"Don't be shy, you've known me since we were twelve! We've shared everything with each other. I haven't seen you look this relaxed in ages. Now, tell me all!"

"You first..." I stood my ground, wanting to keep my private moments with Matt to myself for a bit longer. "What were you muttering about when you rushed in as if the devil were chasing you?"

She sighed. "Sean. Officer Sean, that is, since I broke up with the other one. He won't stop hanging around. The other day he showed up at my door with Chinese food. I didn't want to be rude, since he went to all that trouble, so I invited him in against my better judgment. Damn my parents for having raised me to be polite. I hate to say it, but I actually had a really nice time until he tried to pressure me into letting him sleep over."

"I guess that means he's not working the night shift anymore," I said, remembering that they used to meet for breakfast when they were dating because that's when he was available. Or so he said. Nicole's next comments proved that we had the same doubts.

"I'm not sure he ever did the night shift, to be honest. I don't trust anything he says. When I told him he couldn't stay, he became angry and sort of stormed out. But then this morning, he showed up at the dance studio with coffee from Tim's for me." (Tim's is what we affectionately call our Tim Horton's coffee shop, which Canadians are so fond of even though it's now been sold to Burger King.)

Sean was sounding more and more like a loose cannon to me and I started to worry about Nicole's safety. Could he be her stalker?

"Okay, your turn. Tell me everything!" For a tiny girl, she had a big voice, and my ear drums took the brunt of it.

"Someone slashed my tire, so Matt decided to spend the night to make sure I was safe. I couldn't sleep and uh, well...he ended up in my bed, and let's just say that neither of us got any sleep after that." I blushed.

"He's a keeper, Mali. I could tell right away. Good for you. You wrap those long legs of yours around him and don't let go!"

I grinned at the image and we finished preparing the hot dish, pre-slicing cheeses and meats and lighting the black and red candles on the bistro tables. Nora joined us just before we opened and I noted with relief that she wore a regular bra.

Thankfully, it was a busy but uneventful evening, and before we knew it, we had closed the bistro and were gathered on a couch, each with a glass of red Well Hung in hand. I slapped the bottle down on the table and gestured grandly toward it. "No personal details, ladies, but let's just say that I have no complaints!"

"Is *he* coming tonight?" Nicole teased.

Once our glasses were empty, we decided to call it a night and part ways. On her way out the door Nicole promised to be careful, and Nora and I made our way upstairs as my phone rang. I smiled as I answered. "Want company?" Matt purred into my ear.

"I suppose that depends on who it would be. Did you have anyone in particular in mind?" I teased.

"How about opening your door? You just might find a handsome fellow in your parking lot."

I waited by the door and Nora called out good night, saying she was exhausted and going straight to bed. "Don't stay up too late," she sang out, smirking, before closing her door.

I let Matt inside, both of us grinning from ear to ear. He had changed since this morning and I noticed that he was now carrying a back pack. "I'm spending the night," he announced.

With wobbly knees, I followed him up the stairs.

EASY CHEESY SHEPPARD'S PIE

(Gluten-free, unless there's gluten in the ketchup but then just don't use ketchup)

- 2 cups mashed potatoes (if you don't know how to make that, recipe will follow)
- 1 small can of corn, drained or about 1 and ½ cups frozen corn
- 1 pound lean or extra lean ground beef (you can use ground chicken or turkey but it's not as yummy)
- ½ teaspoon salt, few shakes of pepper and 1 teaspoon garlic powder
- 2 tablespoons ketchup (optional)
- 1 cup grated cheese of your choice (I like cheddar for this or mozzarella or a mix of both)

Cook beef until it is no longer pink, strain off fat, then add spices listed above and the ketchup. The ketchup gives it a little zing and helps bind the meat a bit.

In an 8-inch casserole dish (or something like that) spread

all of the cooked beef on bottom and top with corn. Overtop the corn layer, spread out your mashed potatoes and then on top of that, spread out the grated cheese. To make it prettier, you can add a few sprinkles of dill weed.

Bake at 350 Celsius for about 30 minutes or until cheese is melted and bubbly or slightly browned.

Mashed potatoes
- 8 regular sized potatoes or more if you want leftovers for another dish
- 1 tablespoon margarine or butter
- ⅓ cup milk or less (start with less, about ¼ cup)
- 1 heaping tablespoon sour cream (I used light)
- Salt and pepper to taste
- Dash or two of garlic powder (not garlic salt) if you want to make it garlicky

Peel the potatoes and cut into cubes. Put in pot and cover with water and add about ½ teaspoon salt. The smaller you cut it, the quicker it cooks.

Boil until cooked (pierce potato with fork and taste). Roughly around 20-25 minutes. Drain and put potatoes back in pot.

Add butter or margarine, milk (start with only about ¼ cup, and more if necessary) and sour cream (optional- I like to use this instead of having to use so much butter and it gives it an extra layer of flavor). Give it a few shakes of salt and pepper- taste after mashing before adding more. This depends on your taste buds.

Mash until it's the way you like. If you like it thinner, add more milk, if you like it thicker, add less milk.

CHAPTER THIRTEEN

I awoke to the feeling of eyes staring at me. I opened one eye cautiously and saw Hummer standing by my head. I opened the other and saw Matt looking at me with a lazy smile on his face. I smiled back. Hummer placed a paw on my face and then walked over my head, finally settling down between us, the bum end in Matt's face. That broke the mood.

"It's almost nine; shouldn't you be getting to work?" I asked Matt.

"Yes," he sighed. "I have to go out of town for a few days to work on a sensitive case so I won't see you. I'm going to miss this." His face appeared over Hummers body and he looked at me longingly.

I grinned devilishly and then climbed out of bed. "I'll make some coffee." I gave a little jiggle for his benefit and laughed. As I turned to leave, he called out.

"Hey, not so fast! Were you going to tell me what happened to your legs? That isn't from us the other night, is it?" he asked.

"That's right, I haven't had a chance to tell you about this," I looked down at my still somewhat bruised and scabby legs. "Honestly, I don't know how it happened, but the day I shopped groceries for my parents, I somehow ended up on top of the grocery cart out in the parking lot." My cheeks flamed red as he burst out laughing. I gave a little pout.

"Maybe I should wrap you in bubble wrap...for your own protection!" I nodded in agreement then left the room to prepare breakfast.

We had coffee and a cheese omelet made with sharp cheddar and dill weed and toasted sour dough bread, one of my favorites. Once breakfast was finished, he prepared to leave and promised to call or text in the coming days. At the door, he turned and backtracked to where I still sat, enjoying my coffee. He dragged me to my feet and gave me a back arching kiss that left me panting. Then he was gone.

I watched him from the window, feeling sadder with each step he took. How had he managed to worm his way into my heart so quickly? Even after he was gone, I continued to stare out the window, trying to determine what these feelings were that I was experiencing. "It must be lust," I grumbled to myself.

For a day in late January, it was surprisingly warm. The snow was melting and dripping from the eaves to form long icicles that glittered in the sun like diamonds. I switched my thoughts to the vagrant, Billy, living outside in the elements and then I remembered Matt's comment that maybe he'd seen something significant on the night of the murder. Of course, it was also possible that he was involved in some way.

This would be a perfect day for a little hike on the trails. If I could track him down, maybe I could find out if he knew anything—he seemed more comfortable when I was alone. He certainly seemed familiar with the comings and goings around my bistro. With my mind made up, I pulled on some yoga pants, a loose sweater, light coat, boots, hat and mitts. I quickly packed Billy a bag of goodies and water and headed off onto the trails.

I was at the halfway point between my house and Joey's before I heard the sound of crunching snow in the distance. I stopped abruptly and the sound stopped a split second later. I waited, motionless, glancing about carefully.

He appeared behind me suddenly, scaring me half to death. "Hey, lady, is that food?"

"Billy, I'm happy I found you. I've been worried!" I exclaimed, relieved that he was okay and doubly relieved that it wasn't someone else who had suddenly appeared behind me.

"Why?" he asked suspiciously, backing away from me slightly.

"Because I know you're out here without proper shelter, and no family, and, of course, with a murderer on the loose... You disappeared so suddenly the other day. Why?"

"They were closing in on me," he whispered, glancing about. "They can't pin me down though; I'm too clever. They get close, but I always get away."

"Who? The murderer?" I asked cautiously.

He shrugged.

"What did you see the night the man was killed, Billy?"

His mouth twitched at the corner. "I can't remember. There were voices outside. I couldn't hear very well. That pig kept grunting." His voice suddenly lowered again as he spoke in a whisper. "I know they were looking for me. They're always watching. I was in the garage with the pig, and then the door opened. I hid underneath one of the blankets. Someone came in. I don't know. I stayed very still and very quiet. I could hear someone moving around and then they left. I waited a while, and when no one came back, I took off."

"Why would someone be looking for you, Billy?"

His expression was nervous as he continued to scan the forest. "They want to know what's in my head. You have to listen to me. I can't stay in one place for long because they'll get me. Can I have the food?" he asked suddenly.

I held the bag out to him and he took it with shaking hands. "Have you seen anyone around the bistro that worries you, Billy?" I tried a different tactic. He stood still, scratching his head, the corner of his mouth twitching again a couple of times.

"Yeah, yeah... Your car... Someone was near your car. They were in a snow suit. I couldn't tell who it was." He glanced around nervously again and started to walk away.

"Do you remember anything else? Was it more like a ski-do suit?" I called out. He shook his head and continued walking and shaking his head while glancing over his shoulder. I didn't know if he was saying no, or saying that he didn't remember. This was frustrating.

I looked around slowly, wondering if we were being watched or if his paranoia was contagious. Since the last time I'd seen him, his mental state had deteriorated, but I thought that I was beginning to understand what might be going on with him, unless he was an incredibly good actor.

I was making my way back to the house but stopped abruptly at the mouth of the trail when I saw my parents' car pull into the lot. I hesitated a second too long and they spotted me. They waved and I pasted a smile onto my face and trudged over to them. When they got out of their car I could immediately sense that something was wrong. "Come on up," I said and hurried up the stairs. Whatever it was, I preferred the sanctity of my home rather than getting into it in the great outdoors where I still felt like I was being watched.

We settled in the living room and I suspected I knew what this was about.

"Amalia, vat you doing now?" My father laced right into me.

"What do you mean?" I asked innocently.

"Neighbours tell us that somebody got killed here again!" I opened my mouth to speak but my dad continued. "Vat you do here that everyone getting killed?

You need safe job."

"I do have a safe job; I serve wine and cheese. How much safer can it get? And we don't know if the man was killed here or elsewhere. I didn't know him. Everyone around town hated him. It seems that he and his wife and his girlfriend and her husband were all here that night, and that's when it happened. It has nothing to doing with me."

He shook his head, repeating my name in disappointment while my mother remained quiet, her eyes wide with worry, making her appear even more owlish than usual.

"Listen, Matt is staying here with me now, so I'm safe." I refrained from mentioning that he was out of town for a while. That was on a need to know basis, and as far as I was concerned, they didn't need to know. Deeply disappointed in me, and also worried, they left shortly thereafter. I shrugged to myself. I was used to it.

Agitated, I paced the room. My eyes fell upon the extra page from the reservation book that I had accidentally photocopied the day after the murder for Officer Sean. A number of weeks back, I'd used the tactic of calling people who'd been at my bistro the night a man was murdered and it resulted in my near death when one of the people on the list thought I was on to him. I wasn't keen for a repeat so I put that idea on the backburner for now, but I was anxious to do something, anything. Nevertheless, I gave the list a cursory glance. Valerie's name jumped out at me.

I drove to Valerie's house, hoping to corner her for another chat. I parked on the street and was just about to get out of my car when I saw the door open and Nancy emerge. I quickly ducked down in my seat, just barely peeking out enough to see.

I'm not sure what I expected to see. A cat fight? Yelling? A stabbing? At the very minimum, some hair-pulling and bitch slapping. But I was shocked when the two hugged before Nancy got into her car and drove away.

I remained inside my car for several minutes, still ducking down as far as I could. I lifted my head just in time to see Valerie get into her car. I waited until she was halfway down the street before I set off in hot pursuit. (Ha! I'd always wanted to use that expression and chortled as I said it to myself.)

I quickly glanced at the time and noted with relief that it was still early afternoon. We drove for about twenty minutes until she finally pulled up to a house in the town adjacent to ours. I continued past the house slowly and was driving by just in time to see the door open. The lady who stood there looked vaguely familiar but I couldn't quite place her.

Valerie looked confused by her presence and I could see her backing away, gesturing with her hands. I stopped a few houses away and watched as the lady with the short, bobbed brown hair starting yelling. I used the power window button to lower a back window and listened shamelessly.

"Leave my husband alone and stop trying to get money out of us and destroying my marriage. If I see you near this house again..." The rest was drowned out by a teenaged kid driving by with a loud French muffler and booming subwoofer that rattled my teeth. Startled, I had hurtled myself low in the seat again, hiding as best I could. By the time I looked out again, Valerie was already getting into her car and driving away.

I resumed my drive down the street for about half a block before I came to a cul-de-sac and had no choice but to turn around and go back. My irritation quickly turned to surprise when I saw Markus leaving the same house.

He peeled out of the driveway, and once again I took off in hot pursuit. This was fun, and I wondered briefly what my dad would think if I got a private investigator job with Matt. I knew the answer already; he would say, "That's stupid!"

My luck quickly fizzled out when he lost me at a red

light. I sighed in frustration, unable to shake the feeling that I was on to something and perturbed that something as pesky as a red light was in my way. I drove aimlessly for a few minutes then made a decision and returned to the house.

Ten minutes had passed and I was hoping she'd calmed down by now. I had to think quick as I had no clue how long Markus would be gone. I parked on the street in front of the house and looked around inside my car for inspiration. Nothing... I turned my attention to my messy purse and ransacked it. Aha! Perfect! I marched to the door with determination.

The door was yanked open and the woman stared at me with rage in her eyes. "What?" she barked, surprised and annoyed by a stranger standing on her doorstep.

"Hello, ma'am, I'm sorry to disturb you. It looks like I've come at a bad time. Are you okay?" I feigned concern. Her eyes welled with tears at the unexpected kindness from a stranger.

"Death," she choked out. "Death of someone I was...close to. That's all. I'm fine, but thank you for asking." Her choice of words intrigued me.

"I'm sorry for your loss. Sometimes it's best to talk to someone rather than keep it all bottled up. Obviously, you had been with or knew this person for a long time to be so upset." I fished for information gently, well aware that I probably sounded snoopy even though I tried not to say it in the form of a question.

"I wasn't with him. Well, I guess maybe I was." Her eyes narrowed. "Who did you say you were?"

"Oh, I'm selling Avon products. My name is Dawn Winters. I just stopped by to offer you a catalogue if you're interested." I offered the catalogue that I'd found in my purse.

"Oh. Well, I'm Cathy. Does Shelly no longer sell Avon in this area? I wondered where she'd been lately." I let her believe that and just smiled, thankful that Shelly hadn't been doing her job properly. "Sure, leave it with me; I'll take a look." She took the catalog and started to close the door.

"Are you sure you'll be okay? You seem awfully upset. I hate to leave you like this." I tried to sound concerned.

She shook her head. "My husband Mark will be home soon, thank you all the same." She closed the door before I could say good-bye.

I walked back to the car, smiling victoriously as another puzzle piece clicked into place. She had looked familiar, and then I had placed her the minute she had referred to her husband Markus, as "Mark". She was the lady I'd seen at the corner grocery store, talking about how Alphie had spit on their pizza when "Markus" had complained about the mixed-up order. There was definitely bad blood between those two.

Now what was it again that she had screamed at Valerie? Something about money... And in my brief conversation with her, she had indicated that she and Alphie had been together as a couple, although I was getting the impression that it had not been for long. And I assumed that the death she was referring to was, of course, Alphie! *O, what a tangled web we weave when first we practice to deceive...* And the tangled web was growing! I drove back to the town of Robin and started to get ready for opening at the *Whine*.

CHAPTER FOURTEEN

Chloé arrived just a few minutes before opening time looking dolled up and wearing killer six-inch heels. I grinned to myself, remembering my earlier image of her on a ski-do with her heels.

Like all my other close friends, Chloé was tiny, but unlike the others, she had a serious shoe collection, most of them with impressive heels. These were particularly sexy and I noted she had taken the time to straighten her curly black hair and may have had just a touch more make-up on than usual.

"Do you have a date after work?" I asked curiously, nodding at her heels.

"Nope, but I'm hoping to have one before the night is over!"

"Aha! That's it, you're hoping that ski-do crowd is going to come by tonight, aren't you? You liked that guy that tried to calm the loudmouth, Markus, down. Did you get his name?"

"Yes, it's Jeff, and he's definitely coming tonight, even if the rest of them aren't. He asked me if I'd be working tonight, and when I said yes, he said he'd see me then!"

Her cheeks flushed. Like Nicole, she hadn't had much luck with guys, but she was just barely twenty. She had plenty of frogs to kiss before she'd find her prince.

She'd set about lighting the candles, and I was just putting the Cranberry Almond Bake in the oven when Nicole burst in looking like she hadn't slept in a week. In retrospect, I guess it probably was about a week at this point. "What's wrong?" I got right to the point.

"I didn't sleep again. Between the calls and someone always showing up at my door..." Her voice trailed off as she chewed her bottom lip to stop it from quivering.

"Why don't you sleep here tonight? Nora's going to be at Leonardo's so you can sleep in her bed. If she ends up coming home, you can switch to the couch. Either way, at least you'll get some sleep. My PJs will fit you, as long as you don't mind them being a bit long."

She threw her arms around me. "What a great idea! But won't I get in the way of you and Matt? No offence, but I don't want to overhear you guys!" She wiggled her eyebrows at me and I swatted at her playfully in return.

"He's out of town for a couple of days, so I'm all yours. You can stay as long as you need to, even once he's back. But you really should report this. Do you think the phone calls and the visits are from the same person?"

She nodded. "I'm pretty sure it's Officer Sean. I know I have to do something, but I'm just not sure what. How do you report a cop to the cops?"

I thought about it for a moment and grabbed the notepad that I always had on my counter so that I can write myself to-do lists and ideas whenever the mood hit. I jotted furiously while Nicole watched. "I have a few ideas," I said.

"Yeah, I can see that, Sherlock," she replied.

"Is that any way to talk to your best friend?" I said with equal sarcasm. "We'll talk later." I smacked her with a dish towel, something she'd recently done to me when I had my concussion and she'd shooed me away.

114

As she walked toward the bistro area, Nora came down the inner stairway. I smelled tangerines before I heard or saw her and was sniffing the air when she emerged from the stairs. I looked at her curiously and sniffed my way over to her. "Did you rub yourself with tangerines or oranges?" I asked.

"Body spray," she replied, looking smug and batting her eyelashes. "See you tomorrow. I'll bring some food to Chicha and then I'm off." Armed with a bag of treats for the pig, she was gone.

I took the desserts out of the oven so they could cool and picked at a partially loose hot almond, my mouth pooling with anticipation. I couldn't wait for a big bite but sadly I would have to. Customers were starting to arrive.

It was a Friday night, and since the weather was mild, people were out and about. It was busier than we had expected and we dashed about at double time to keep up with the demand. It was about eight o'clock and Nicole was just taking the stage at the piano when the ski-do gang started to pile in, distinctive in their snow-mobiling gear. I counted seven of them today, and Markus was not among them.

I saw Chloé burst out in her goofy grin and knew that Jeff had arrived. I saw their eyes seek out each other before a conversation caught my ear and distracted me. I moved toward the table I was serving with more wine.

They had left the choice to me, and I poured the two men and two women—all dressed in jeans and brightly colored plaid shirts—some Redneck Red. My ears perked up as I unabashedly listened in on their conversation.

"I borrowed money from him once and let me tell you, I sure regretted it. The bank had turned us down for a loan and I needed to get the tractor fixed. He was real nice about it but when it came time for me to pay him back, he told me he had to adjust the interest rate since the markets were bad and he had taken a hard hit. I had to pay him a hundred more each month than he originally said. When I said there's no way interest rates should result in that much of an increase, he started talking about his connections and how the matter can be solved some other way. I didn't want to know how so I just shut up and paid and never dealt with him again."

"You got off lucky," his buddy replied. "I was still paying him back for a loan and he kept asking for more each month..." He broke off as his wife shushed him. I busied myself at the table next to them, wiping it sparkling clean and re-arranging the stools around it. They spoke in lower voices and I only caught the odd word.

"Threatening...bastard would...and then he... off at the knees..." My frustration grew. I hurried back to the kitchen and sliced thin pieces of Cranberry Almond Bake then arranged them on a number of plates, topping each with a dollop of whipped cream. Then I went back to their table.

"May I offer you a free sample of my latest treat?"

Each accepted. Then the woman who'd hushed her husband earlier said, "This is fantastic! Can I order a big piece to go, please?" The other lady also requested more while the two men asked for more wine, a glass of white this time, something on the sweet side.

"May I suggest a dessert wine? I have something that will go perfectly with the sweets." All four nodded and I soon returned with two desserts in 'to go' containers and four glasses of Inniskillin Ice wine. I had bought a couple of bottles for the bistro after having fallen in love with it myself. I grinned as all four sets of eyes rolled back in pleasure after a first tentative sip. This was my chance to get them while they were weak.

"I don't mean to be rude, but I heard some of your conversation earlier. Can I assume you were talking about Alphie?" My inquiry was greeted with somber silence. But I continued. "I've run into a few people who just couldn't stand him, and of course you know that he was found in my garage. I'm just trying to figure out why he was killed here."

Taking pity on me, one of the men finally broke his silence. "I wouldn't take it personally, Miss. There's probably no connection to your place other than someone finally got him alone in the dark and took advantage of it. He wasn't a nice person. He even put the squeeze on his own uncle after giving him a loan for that pizza joint at the corner." My eyes widened in surprise.

"Mr. Leonardo?" I asked. He nodded.

"He sounds like a real snake. I've heard that he often threatened people. Do you know if it's true that he had *connections*?"

The men shrugged. "He threatened everyone. I'm not sure anyone challenged him since they didn't want to find out if he really did have, as you say, *connections*. I know I didn't!"

His wife shot him another dirty look. "Shush, Frank. People will think that you wanted him dead. You paid him back every dime, and then we stayed away from him." This last bit was aimed in my direction.

One of the ladies murmured quietly, "Everyone wanted him dead, dear. The only question is, who wanted him dead the most?" They laughed nervously then changed the subject. I went back to the kitchen to jot down my notes then I peeked out at Chloé.

She'd made the rounds with the customers and was now at the ski-do table. They had all ordered the daily hot dish, which was stuffed pasta shells. She was talking with a cute, brown haired guy that I assumed was Jeff. She looked up to catch me watching and gave me the one-minute signal.

She joined me in the kitchen. "I have a date!" she squealed. "I'm going ski-doing with him after I finish here tonight."

"In the dark?" I asked, suddenly nervous for her. Someone from that gang could be the killer.

"Don't worry; the ski-do has lights. We're just going across a flat field for a little ride, and if I like it, he invited me to ride with them tomorrow during the day." She was clearly excited and I didn't want to be a downer, but I couldn't hide my anxiety even though this was exactly what I hoped would happen.

"Just be careful, okay? One of them could be the killer, since Alphie was killed the night they were all here. If you can do it cautiously though, maybe try to find out a bit more about why Markus hated Alphie so much, since he was so verbal about it the other night."

She nodded, "I'm on it. Um, now that things are starting to wind down, do you think I can sneak out a tiny bit early?"

I smiled, feeling her excitement. "Of course. Nicole and I can close; she's sleeping over tonight anyway."

I brought the bill to the table of four that I'd spoken with earlier and ventured a bit more conversation. "A friend of mine is dating Mr. Leonardo. You mentioned that even he owed Alphie money. I don't know him very well, but he's always seemed very volatile and angry with me...would you say my friend could be in danger?"

They exchanged glances before one of the men spoke. "If it was my friend, I'd try to fix her up with someone else. He doesn't exactly have the best reputation around town...just like his nephew."

I scanned the crowd. I'm not sure what I was expecting, but as if on cue, the front door opened and in walked Craig, Nora's husband. He had always been a thin man, but he seemed to have lost weight. He had dark circles underneath his eyes. His reddish hair was a bit wild and his coppery beard needed a trim. I greeted him warmly and he returned my hug but declined my offer of a drink. "I was hoping to see Nora," he said shyly. "Would you mind telling her that I'm here?"

"I'm sorry, Craig, but she's out with some friends this evening," I lied smoothly to spare his feelings. He didn't need to know about Mr. Leonardo. "I'm not sure if she's coming back tonight; she mentioned something about a possible sleepover. I'll be sure to tell her you stopped by though."

"Thanks," he said.

"Would you like something to eat?" I offered.

"I'm not really hungry these days. I'll just go back home. Thank you, Amalia." He left the bistro in despair and my heart went out to him. I'd have to talk some sense into Nora.

Half an hour later, Nicole and I locked up and dragged ourselves upstairs to the living quarters. While she took a shower, I put fresh sheets on Nora's bed, fixed us a snack and poured us each a fishbowl size glass of Dark Side of the Moon. The wine matched my mood. It seemed like everyone in this town had a dark side these days.

Nicole ambled out of the bathroom with her pajama bottoms rolled up and flopping around her ankles due to our difference in height. She joined me on the couch and wordlessly showed me her phone and how many missed calls she had, presumably all from Sean, caller ID blocked. I checked my own phone. There was no word from Matt yet.

"I have a germ of a plan," I started, as we both took a huge gulp of wine. "When he calls, answer and put him on speaker phone like you did the other day. I'll record it with my phone. Each time he calls, answer, and that's what we'll do. Then we'll be able to show what a psycho he is. When Matt's back, I'll play the recordings for him and he can help us figure out what to do next. He was a cop, after all, so he should know the proper way to go about reporting another cop for misconduct or stalking or whatever he's doing."

She nodded, "Great thinking!" As if right on cue, her phone rang and we both jumped and yelped in surprise. "Here we go," she said as I scrambled for my phone. I nodded to indicate I was in record mode.

"Hello?" she answered sweetly.

"Where are you?" the Voice barked.

"Good evening, Officer Sean. To what do I owe this honor at eleven-thirty at night?"

"I knocked on your door. Why didn't you answer?"

"I must have been in the shower," she lied smoothly, not wanting him to know where she was. "Why would you knock on my door, Sean? We broke up a while ago, though you refuse to accept it. Why don't you go back to the other woman in your life?"

"I told you, she's just a roommate. I thought we could hang out tonight. I mean, I was hoping we could. Come on, baby."

"Sean, just like I've been telling you every night for the past few nights, no. Please leave me alone and stop calling me so many times a day and texting me and coming by my place or my work. I'd hate to have to file harassment charges against you."

He swore like a sailor, calling her every unpleasant name in the book. We covered our mouths with our hands to stop ourselves from laughing out loud. This recording would certainly not paint a very nice picture of him.

When he was done, Nicole spoke: "I don't understand, Sean; you always say such mean things, but then you want to come see me. This is very confusing, and you're scaring me. I'd like you to leave me alone, please, and forget about me. Stop calling, stop texting and stop showing up at my work. I'm hanging up now."

She hung up and I stopped the recording before we burst into laughter.

"Oh, my gosh, that was great, Nicole! He played right into your..." I stopped as her phone rang again. She nodded; it was him again. I nodded back when I activated the record option.

This went on for a few more phone calls before Nicole finally put her foot down. "Listen, Sean, I'm going to bed now. I'm turning off my phone. Leave me alone."

She really did turn off her phone, and we drained our glasses and called it a night.

I was just about to doze off when I heard two shrieks from down the hall. I lurched out of bed and fell to the floor when one foot remained trapped in the blankets. I did a worm-like move to free myself, felt around for the baseball bat that I keep under my bed and ran to the spare room. The sounds of hysterical laughter greeted me as I approached. I lowered my bat and listened, cautiously advancing. Was an intruder tickling Nicole?

I stood in the doorway, the corners of my lips twitching. Nicole had shed my too-large pajamas and was naked in the bed, the blanket now firmly held in place to cover her boobs. Nora, on the other hand, was sitting on the bed in an orange push up bra and matching thong underwear. Both were laughing and had tears streaming down their faces. Upon seeing my surprised expression, they laughed even harder. Between shrieks of laughter I was able to piece the details together.

Leonardo had been snoring as loud as a freight train and Nora had finally snapped. Faced with the decision of covering his face with a pillow or returning home, she'd opted for home. She hadn't turned on any lights and was unaware that Nicole was sleeping in her bed until she crawled in next to her. That was when both of them had yelped.

"I'll fix up the couch for one of you. I'll let you two decide which of you is sleeping on it," I said and went off in search of more bedding. Nicole came out of the room wearing the PJs again, still laughing. She caught my eye and mouthed, "Thong!" and again we had to cover our mouths to stop ourselves from laughing. I was as surprised as she was by Nora's attire. I did, however, really like the color. The old bird had good taste.

We all attempted to get back to sleep. I could hear Nicole toss and turn on the couch and then I heard a soft snoring from down the hallway and started giggling again. Nora had come home because Leonardo was snoring, but yet she too snored. Once I heard Nicole giggling from the living room, I couldn't contain myself any longer. Then, upon hearing me laugh, her giggles grew even louder. "Go to sleep!" I called out. This was like our sleepovers in our teens. It took a while, but our giggles eventually died down and I finally drifted off.

CRANBERRY ALMOND BAKE

- 1 and ½ cups white granulated sugar
- ¾ cup melted butter or margarine (if you used sticks of butter that's 1 and ½)
- 2 large eggs
- ½ block of light cream cheese, softened (leave on counter a couple of hours or soften in the microwave for 20 seconds or so)
- 1 and 2/3 cups white flour
- 1 tablespoon pure Almond extract
- 1 good squeeze of lemon juice
- 1 cup sliced almonds
- ½ cup dried cranberries or candied cherries
- 2 tablespoons white granulated sugar

Melt butter or margarine and remove from heat. Allow to cool for 5 minutes. Add 1 and ½ cups sugar and mix. Next add eggs, cream cheese, lemon juice and almond extract and mix again. Add flour, mix until smooth although there may be some cream cheese bits. That's okay. Add cranberries and mix.

123

Take a cast iron skillet and line it with aluminum foil including up the sides of the skillet. I put the shiny side up. Spray with cooking spray. Pour in batter. Top with sliced almonds so that the top is evenly covered and then sprinkle with 2 tablespoons sugar.

Bake at 350 degrees Celsius (or 325 if your oven cooks fast) for about 35 minutes or until the almonds are a nice toasty color. Be sure not to burn it. Remove and let cool in pan. When cool enough to handle, lift out with the foil and place on a plate until cool enough to cut into wedges. Delicious warm or cold, on its own, or topped with custard, vanilla pudding or whipped cream. Or all of the above all at once.

CHAPTER FIFTEEN

I was the first one awake the next day, once again up early. I was getting awfully bitter about not having my lazy mornings. Full of energy but not wanting to wake Nora or Nicole, I snuck out the door by nine, having run out of things to do that didn't make noise.

First stop, Walmart. Luckily for me there was a sale on bedding, and I stocked up on blankets and sheets then picked up some groceries and headed back home. I was almost there when I realized that I'd forgotten to go to the liquor store. I had been on the hunt for the Fifty Shades of Gray wine that I needed for my Valentine's Day display. I decided to stop in at the local liquor store in Robin, located in the same shopping complex as the pizza place and post office. I wasn't optimistic that they would have it but didn't feel like backtracking.

I glanced quickly at my watch. It was eleven and the post office was only open until noon since it was a Saturday. Deciding that I should stop there first, I took a deep breath, pasted on a smile and walked in. Nancy was not happy to see me.

"What now?" she groaned. "Why can't you just leave

125

me alone?"

"Hi, Nancy, good to see you too. Listen, I was visiting my parents yesterday and just happened to drive past Valerie's house as you were leaving. I saw you two hugging. I was surprised since you mentioned that you and Alphie had been together for the past year, and because she's his widow."

She fidgeted nervously with some bubble wrap. Pop. Pop. The first pop had caught me by surprise and I jumped, stirring my slumbering aneurism in the process. Okay, so I don't really have one, it's just what I fondly call the stabbing pain I sometimes get above my left eyebrow. It strikes suddenly but doesn't usually last more than a few seconds. This time it didn't subside.

"Valerie and I are friends," she sighed. "We go way back. I knew her before she ever got married."

"Did she know about you and Alphie?" I asked.

She shook her head no. "I don't think so. Can we not talk about it anymore, please? I really have nothing more to say. I don't know why you keep sticking your nose into it, anyway." She had me there.

"I'm just trying to help clear all this up," I mumbled, and with nothing more to say, I left, but not before I noticed that her hand still had a big Band-Aid on it.

I was rubbing my left temple and was preoccupied with my thoughts as I hurried into the liquor store. I gasped in surprise when I came face to face with Matt near the check- out counter. "Matt!" I exclaimed, my joy fading quickly once I took note of his arm that was around a lanky, sandy-haired beauty.

"Malia! I guess you caught me red-handed," he chuckled without shame, making no attempt to remove his arm.

Speechless from shock, I turned and ran from the store. I could hear him calling my name but I didn't stop. I ran blindly to my car and peeled out of the lot. I figured he'd come to the house soon enough if he had the balls to break up with me officially, and I really didn't want to deal with it, so I drove over to the next town and had a coffee at a Tim's. And a Boston cream donut. And an apple fritter. Finally, a sour cream glazed donut. Once the feeling of nausea outweighed the feeling of sadness, I returned home, heartbroken and fat.

Both Nora and Nicole were up when I walked into the living room and looked at me curiously as I entered. Nicole was the first to speak.

"Matt was here. He said he really needs to speak to you and he looked very upset. What happened?"

A single tear managed to escape despite my best effort to contain it. "I saw him at the liquor store. With his arm around another woman. When he was supposed to be out of town for a few days." I choked the words out around the lump in my throat.

"There must be a good explanation," Nora said. "He wouldn't do that right here in Robin, right under your nose. He doesn't seem like the type that would do that at all, and I've seen the way he looks at you," she insisted.

"Why not? It seems like everyone around here cheats on each other," I said bitterly. "Anyway, I don't want to talk to him, or about him. I'm going down to the bistro to start preparing for tonight. Speaking of cheating, Nora, Craig came by to see you last night. He didn't look too good." She didn't respond but I could see her mouth fly open in response to my bitchiness and callous choice of words. I instantly regretted it but there was no taking it back. I slunk out of the room feeling lower than a slug.

I deliberately left my cell phone in my room. I could see he'd already texted me but I was too sad and too mad to deal with his excuse. He gotten what he'd wanted, and now he was on to his next conquest. Maybe he'd been with her all along. I pushed my thoughts aside and turned my focus to getting the hot dish ready. Chloé was the first to arrive, and Nicole and Nora came downstairs just moments later.

We still had an hour before we were due to open. I could tell that Chloé was bursting with news and I pasted what I hoped would pass for a smile onto my face.

"So?" I prompted.

"Jeff is so nice," she gushed. "Oh, and Markus was there today. He is not a happy camper, and he is rude with everyone. I did learn something new, though. Alphie was a loan shark. Half the guys in the ski-do crowd owed him money. Jeff was telling me how one guy got into a fist fight with Alphie not long before he was killed. That guy hasn't been seen since. Jeff has tried to call him, but there's been no answer."

"Good work Chloé! Jeff didn't wonder why you were asking all these questions, did he?" Nicole asked worriedly.

"I didn't even have to ask. He volunteered all this information. He said Markus and Alphie had plenty of bad chemistry, and he suspects that Markus may have been sneaking around with Alphie's wife, but he wasn't sure."

"Oh, he was," I confirmed. "Leonardo told me about that."

"*My* Leo?" Nora exclaimed. "When did you talk to Leo? And how is it that you are still alive?"

I laughed at the surprise on her face. I hadn't had a chance to tell her about the conversation, or to share my findings with anyone. "Yes, we spoke the other day when I told him that Valerie was being followed. That's the only reason he was willing to listen. So here's what we have. Alphie was sleeping with Nancy and used to sleep with another woman named Cathy. Cathy is married to Markus. Markus slept with Valerie. Nancy and Valerie were friends. Valerie and Cathy are definitely not friends and there was something about money involved, possibly blackmail. It also turns out that Alphie was putting the squeeze on Leonardo for money," I revealed as I glanced at Nora. "And that means that you might not be safe, since Leonardo also appears to be somehow involved. He could even be the killer." I allowed myself a brief but delicious moment to fantasize and picture him apprehended and behind bars. Someone else would have to run the pizza shop, and then I could finally eat there.

Nora's eyes were shining. "Oh boy, you sure found out a lot! I missed out on all this? That's it; I'm spending more time with you from now on. Anyway, it was fun to have a little fling, but I'm not sure that Leo's the one for me."

We all waited for her to continue. "Why not?" I finally asked.

"Well, the snoring, for one thing. Plus, he spits in the sink." She shuddered. "I can't stand that—big turn off. And he has hair on his back. It's like snuggling with a shaggy rug." We all nodded in sympathy and bit our lips to keep from laughing.

"You do know that Leonardo was dating the former owner's wife, don't you, Nora? Nicole and I saw them together a few weeks ago; they were in a restaurant downtown getting cozy with each other." The former owners of the building I now owned had come by to check out the bistro shortly after I opened it. The wife and I had talked briefly about Mr. Leonardo, and she had shared that he had once wandered upstairs while she was in the bath. I had correctly suspected at the time that there was more to that story.

Nora's head snapped in my direction and there was almost a look of relief upon her face. "Well, that explains the silky robe in his bathroom then. And I was starting to wonder if he was some kind of weirdo!" She cackled loudly.

"Alright then, let's open," I said, once I trusted myself to speak.

Out of habit, I normally peek out the window before unlocking the doors. Admittedly, I was distracted and, quite frankly, I was still picturing Mr. Leonardo wearing a silky robe on his hairy back and imagining it shedding onto his pizzas. With this image in mind, I unlocked and whipped open the door for a breath of fresh air to clear my head.

And came face to face with Hans and his perfectly styled blond hair. Woe is me! Today, I was in no mood to be polite.

"To what do I owe the displeasure this time?" I snarled, obviously not letting him inside.

"Can't I just come in for a glass of wine? Maybe a glass of Sassy Bitch?" he replied.

"No, you can listen to this sassy bitch 'whine' out here. I'm tired of you lurking about. If you come here one more time, I will get a restraining order against you. Does this visit have a purpose, or are you just harassing me?"

He sneered. "Where's your boyfriend? Are you going to send him after me again?" Hans was referring to an incident a few weeks ago when Matt had exchanged words with him and sent him on his way.

"That all depends . Are you going to keep pestering me? And why were you in my bistro the other day?" It still bothered me that he'd been inside.

"I just heard that you had another murder here not long ago. Guess everyone's dying to get in, eh?"

"You're a barrel of laughs. Did you come just to gloat, or are you confessing to murder? If I recall correctly, you were here the night that it happened." I gave him a beady-eyed look to imply that I might hold him personally responsible.

He tried to look tough. "Maybe a bit of both. What do you think of that? Maybe you should be careful. It might be you next time."

His tough boy act didn't work with me. "Get lost!" I slammed the door in his face and turned to find Nicole, Nora and Chloé standing behind me in solidarity.

"What the hell was that about?" Nora demanded.

"Every now and then he just likes to torment me. As if living with him for six years wasn't torture enough. Now that I have the bistro, I'm sure that he thinks he can get some money out of me. Maybe he figures that if he irritates me enough, I might pay him to stay away. Plungerhead!" Incidentally, Plungerhead was also a wine, and I took a second to smirk to myself.

There were definitely no lingering feelings of affection for Hans. I had lived with him all those years, repeatedly breaking up and taking him back. When I found a condom in his wallet, I knew it was time to move on. Since we were in what I thought was an exclusive relationship, we didn't use condoms, so I knew it wasn't for my benefit.

"I bet he's still sitting out there in his car, laughing at me. He thinks he intimidates me." I snatched the door open again to glare into the parking lot.

And came face to face with Matt. And the leggy, sandy-haired lady I'd seen him with earlier. And he still had an arm around her! Was I really just a Miss Wednesday night to him? I counted the days backwards and groaned to myself. Crap! I had first slept with him on a Wednesday night! How stupid could I have been?

The first two times I'd met him, he was with a different woman each time. When he asked me out, I figured he just wanted to add a third to his harem, and that he just happened to have an opening on Wednesday nights. He claimed that they were blind dates and that he wasn't a womanizer, but clearly he had been lying.I glared at him and put my hands on my hips. "I've just finished dealing with one cheating bastard, and now here's another. What are you doing here?" I spat.

"This is my sister, Gracie," Matt said quickly before I could slam the door.

I suddenly felt like a balloon with the air leaking out. "Oh," I said, surprised. "Oh," I repeated, totally embarrassed. "OH!" I exclaimed, excited and throwing myself into his arms.

Then I stepped away, the embarrassment quickly returning. "I'm so sorry," I apologized, trying to hide my flaming cheeks behind my long hair. "I was taken by surprise, and when I saw Matt's arm around you, I just assumed... well, I assumed the wrong thing, obviously. But Matt, what did you mean when you said that I caught you red-handed? And might I remind you that you were supposed to be out of town? I certainly hadn't heard from you." The anger was returning, and as I proceeded to make a spectacle of myself, I was thankful that we didn't have any other customers yet.

"Why don't we go inside and sit down and then I'll explain," Matt replied, as a couple of cars pulled into the lot, right on cue.

The three of us settled onto one of the couches, and Nicole brought us a bottle of wine and three glasses. I chuckled when I noticed the name of the wine; Oops! This was an *oops* moment, all right!

Matt pulled me close for a hug before explaining. "I finished the job sooner than expected and I was back yesterday but I got in late. I had ordered a special wine for you and I had a message that the order was in, so I met my sister, who lives close by, for brunch and then we went to pick up your present. That's what I meant when I said you caught me red-handed, because I was just on my way to the check-out with it."

Gracie struggled with a bag then held it out for me. Hearing the clink of bottles, I shyly accepted and thanked her. I opened it and smiled. It was six bottles of the Fifty Shades that I'd been searching for. I apologized again and Matt leaned over to whisper to me. "Don't worry, I can think of a few ways for you to make it up to me."

"Hey you too, I'm still here, hello," his sister joked.

"By the way, is it my imagination or was that your ex I saw driving away when I arrived?" Matt asked, changing the subject.

"Came by to let me know he's still breathing, I guess."

I left the two of them to enjoy their drinks and the platter of cheeses that Nicole had also brought. It was time to work as the customers were beginning to come in now.

At some point his sister left, but Matt hung out with me in the kitchen or sat at the bar when I was busy.

With only ten minutes left until closing time, I suddenly felt my hackles rise. Figuratively, of course. I turned, scanning the crowd. The ski-doers were all here, as was Markus, but he was quite subdued this evening and had not even glanced in my direction. Aside from that there were a couple of regulars just getting ready to leave, a couple of strangers settling their bill and...Officer Sean. I froze.

Pasting a smile on my face, I rushed over to him. "Officer Sean, how nice to see you again. Are you on duty?"

"No, where's Nicole?"

"Come over to the bar and let me pour you a glass of wine on the house. You prefer red, right?" I seated him and poured him a glass of Bad Attitude. "So tell me, how's the investigation going? Has the killer been found yet? Do we know what the murder weapon was? Any leads? I found out that he was a loan shark and that there are several people with a motive. We should really compare notes. When can we do that? Should I come down to the station tomorrow?" I bombarded him with questions, hoping to drive him away before Nicole saw him.

He raised his brow, scrutinizing me and finally deciding there was no getting rid of me. This was my turf, after all.

"You are correct. There were quite a number of people who wanted him dead, so we're chasing down all the leads, which takes time. Other than what I told you the other day, we still don't know exactly how he was killed—no weapon. There seems to be an entry wound but no signs of exit. Is Nicole here?" He asked again, more politely this time.

"I'm not sure; she might have left already, but I'll check for you shortly. Just a couple more things, if you don't mind: Is it true that Alphie had mob ties?"

He sighed as though I'd just asked him to solve the

Rubik's cube. "As you mentioned earlier, he was a loan shark, but no, he didn't have connections, at least not that we are able to determine. He was just a two-bit weasel and pretended he was with the Mafia to make people afraid of him and do what he wanted them to do. Anything else?"

"Yes, thanks for asking, just one more thing..." I was just about to tell him about Billy and what he may have seen that night when he was in my garage, but then suddenly thought better of it. "You know what, I'll go see if Nicole's here."

I went back to the kitchen where she was finishing tidying up. "Where's Matt?" I asked.

"He went upstairs. He said he was going to get a snack ready for you," she replied. "Is that your code word for sex?" She started tp laugh and I quickly shushed her, clamping my hand over her mouth.

"Listen to me. Go up and join him right now. Sean is here. I'll tell him you've already left. It's a good thing you parked your car out back where no one can see it, so he won't know unless he snoops around."

She had a sudden look of panic and then bolted up the stairs. I waited a couple of minutes then I went back to where Sean was sitting.

"Sorry, she's already left. She mentioned that she might slip out early. The poor thing hasn't been sleeping well lately. Some psychopath has been harassing her. Hey, do you think she should file a complaint? Can that be investigated somehow even though the caller information was blocked?"

He gave no outward signs of panic at my onslaught of questions, and had I not been watching closely, I would have missed the slight tightening of his lips.

"Unless she's been threatened in some way there's not much chance that anything would be done. I should probably swing by her place and make sure she's safe though." After throwing a few bills on the bar, he quickly left. I breathed a sigh of relief and locked the door.

134

The only guest left inside the bistro was Chloé's new beau, Jeff. She was sitting on a couch with him and they were talking softly while Nora was wiping down tables. Seeing that we were now officially closed, Chloé and Jeff stood and walked over to me. She introduced us and Jeff shook my hand, but as I drew mine away, I noticed something red. "Oh, I'm bleeding!" I inspected my hand but there didn't appear to be a cut.

"I'm sorry, that's me," Jeff replied. "I've had a cut for a while and it keeps opening up and bleeding." He lifted his hand and dabbed at his wrist with a napkin from the bar. I studied him closely for a moment before speaking.

"My condolences for the recent loss. How long did you know Alphie?"

"About four years now. Ever since he started ski-doing with us, I guess."

"Did you get along with him?"

Chloé glared at me but I ignored her.

"No one really got along with him. You either put up with him, ignored him, or catered to him if you owed him something. I put up with him, but then again, I can tolerate most people. He was a challenge though, that's for sure." He had answered my question pleasantly enough but I noticed a slight tightening around his eyes.

"I'm guessing you didn't owe him money then? Or sleep with his wife?" I blurted this out and earned another glare from Chloé. I'd have to be careful so that she didn't kick me with her killer heels next comment. "Sorry, I'm just hearing things around town and I want to make sure that my friend here is safe, that's all. Please don't take offence," I said sweetly, giving him a hundred-watt smile. I had just used some tooth whitening strips that morning, in fact, so my smile must have been particularly dazzling. "Your cut is a real gusher. How did it happen?" I handed him more napkins and watched him carefully.

"You sure get right to the point, don't you?" he said, immune to my smile. "No, I didn't owe him money; no, I didn't sleep with his wife, and the cut is a scratch from my cat. Your friend is perfectly safe with me. Now then, shall we?" he said, turning to Chloé, perhaps a bit miffed but making a good attempt a hiding it. She, however, glared daggers at me.

I let them out the back door since Chloé had to go to the office area for her winter coat. While they walked around the side of the house to the front, I dashed across the bistro to peer out the blinds, turning the lights out along the way.

"What are you doing?" Nora asked, making me jump. I had totally forgotten about her and had plunged her into darkness.

"Just watching. I'm not so sure about Jeff," I whispered, although there was no way they could hear me from outside. I watched as he walked her to her car, kissed her for a few seconds, and then walked to his car. Just before getting inside, he lifted his head and looked toward the bistro. Even from the distance, he appeared angry.

"Well, well, well... Do we have ourselves another suspect?" I mused out loud. "Who *did* you sleep with, Jeff? Was I right? Was it with Alphie's wife? I *will* find out. You're involved in this triangle too, aren't you?" By now I'd come to suspect that everyone here was connected by their private parts, and my love triangle theory now seemed more like a hexagon. Prying myself away from the window, Nora and I then trudged upstairs to find Matt and Nicole waiting for us.

"I told Matt everything about Sean," she said. "He just needs to hear the recordings you made." I got my cell phone and played back the recordings for Matt and Nora to hear.

Nora was the first to speak. "The night I slept there, was it him that kept calling then too?"

Nicole nodded. "Yeah, I'm pretty sure it was."

"So much for relying on cops to keep us safe."

Matt looked grim. "Play it again, Malia," he instructed,

putting his own phone in record mode. He recorded my recordings and they turned out surprisingly good. "I've got some contacts at the police department still. Leave this with me for a few days. We'll take Nicole to her place tomorrow for a change of clothes." She was wearing her jeans with one of my sweaters today, but my pants wouldn't fit her, nor would any of my underclothes. "I guess I'll head home now," he said reluctantly, rising from the couch.

"What is this, the nineteen forties?" Nora laughed. "For heaven's sake, stay the night Matt. We're all adults. Anyway, I'm sure we'd all agree that we'll feel much safer knowing that you're here."

He stood awkwardly by the door, undecided.

I smiled and wiggled my eyebrows. "May as well stay, Matt. Let's have a snack."

CHAPTER SIXTEEN

We lay face to face for a few minutes, staring at each other awkwardly. He felt strange with my two friends so close by, and I was still embarrassed over how I'd reacted earlier when I assumed he'd cheated on me. If I were honest with myself, I also had to admit that I was surprised by the amount it had hurt since the relationship was still quite new. I hadn't intended to care for him so much, at least not so soon, and it freaked me out a little. Drained, we snuggled up together and were both soon asleep. Hummer showed his displeasure by choosing to sleep with Nicole.

Not more than an hour later, we heard pounding at the front door. Matt was the first out of bed and was already at the bedroom door before I'd even lifted my head off the pillow. "I'll check it out," he said, and then I heard him in the living room talking to Nicole. "I'll get it, Nicole; you go to the room with Malia." Whoever was at the door was still pounding, not having paused for a polite break. I joined Nicole in the living room, neither of us intending to hide.

He looked out the peephole. "It's Sean." Nicole looked at me wildly then ran to the bathroom while I joined Matt at the door.

"Evening, Officer, what brings you here at this time of night? Has something happened?" Matt asked politely and with just the right amount of concern to his tone. Sean was completely taken aback by Matt's presence and was speechless for several heartbeats.

"Uh, Matt? What are you... oh...I see. I was looking for Nicole. I noticed that her car is parked in the back. I was concerned when I found out that someone was after her and she hasn't been home, so I thought I'd come back here to see if she was spending the night. I just want to make sure she's safe."

He turned to look at me. "Is Nicole's car parked in the back?"

"I suppose it could be. But she's not here, Sean. As you know, she left a bit early today and probably caught a ride with a friend. I didn't realize she wasn't taking her car."

He reluctantly left, but not before glancing around. His gaze fell upon the blanket on the couch and Matt noticed. "Amalia's friend Nora is staying here so I was sleeping on the couch." Sean raised a brow but didn't comment.

Next morning we were having breakfast when someone knocked at the door again. Expecting it to be Sean, Nicole once again hid in the bathroom as Matt approached the door and peered out. "Oops. It's for you, Amalia. *Bazd meg!*" He grinned as he used the Hungarian swear words that he'd heard me say on a number of occasions.

"No!" I gasped. "My parents?"

He nodded. "Shall I hide in the bathroom with Nicole?"

"No. I told them if they see cars in the lot not to call unexpectedly." I marched to the door and greeted them. They peered over my shoulder.

"Ah, Mutt, good seeing you. Ve not staying. Amalia, don't forget on Tuesday you have the dancing class. Mama's decided she's gonna try."

OMG! My mother was coming to the pole dancing class?

"Oh, here is new phone number; we have telephone now." He slipped me a piece of paper and then they were gone.

"Matt, check outside, will you? Tell me, are pigs flying? Do you see Chicha floating in the sky? That was their shortest visit ever and they didn't even say anything about the fact that you obviously slept here."

We finished our breakfast and I quickly threw some ingredients in a couple of slow cookers for tonight's dish, then we drove Nicole home to pack a bag. She froze as she approached her apartment and then burst into tears. Someone had written the word 'bitch' in black permanent marker across the white door. Matt took a picture with his cell phone and Nicole didn't dawdle. We were in and out within minutes.

"I'll see you later," he promised, dropping us off at the bistro and giving me a quick kiss. He had some things to do and I had some leads that I needed to look into so I was relieved that we were parting ways. The less Matt knew, the less he'd get in my way or nag me. Leave it to me to get a boyfriend who used to be a cop and now has his own private investigation firm but didn't want me hunting down clues. You would think he'd be thrilled and would want to take me under his wing and teach me everything he knew. No way!

Nicole went back to bed, still exhausted after all the sleep she'd missed earlier in the week, and I decided to pay a visit to Mr. Leonardo. I went out to my car and stopped in dismay. Damn it! Another tire slashed. However, it appeared to be a different style of vandalism this time, with only a couple of large, deep slashes instead of many smaller ones. What did that mean? Did a different person do it, or was the person just less angry? I had no clue.

I dashed back upstairs to leave Nicole a note that I had to borrow her car and would soon be back. As I opened her car door, I screeched in surprise. Sprawled in the back seat was Billy. He lurched upright and looked about wildly.

"Billy, it's me. You scared me. What are you doing here?"

"You scared me too. Why'd you do that? I was sleeping."

"How did you get in?" I glanced around and didn't notice any broken windows.

"The doors weren't locked. Your friend should be more careful."

"Billy, do you want to come inside for some food?" I was breaking my own rule about not letting him in but by now I was pretty sure I was on the right track and knew what I was dealing with.

He looked at me suspiciously, sizing me up, and then nodded. We went into the bistro's kitchen where I fixed him a sandwich with toasted rye bread, succulent Montreal smoked meat, thin, delicate slices of Asiago cheese and a little mustard. It was gone within minutes. While he was eating I packed him another bag filled with treats.

"Billy, you mentioned the other day that you needed money for medicine. I thought you meant drugs or booze, but I think you really did mean medicine, didn't you?"

He looked around nervously. "I'm gonna go now..."

"Wait! You know we're friends now, right? I wouldn't be trying to help you if I wasn't a friend. Are you familiar with the term schizophrenic?" I asked point blank as he was now getting very fidgety and ready to bolt.

"That's what they say I am. They tell me I need medicine because I don't think like everybody else, but I don't want to think like everybody else and be controlled the way they are. They don't even see how they're just puppets. They say not everyone can hear the voices and that I'm special, but if I take the medicine, I can make the voices quieter. I'm not sure what to believe. Listen, I gotta go now."

Before I could say anything further, he bolted out the

door with his treat bag. I debated calling for help but it was Sunday, so I finally decided that better resources would be available on a weekday and a couple of more days wouldn't matter. Was it my responsibility to get involved? Truth be told, I was worried about him.

I went back out to the car, and once on the road I noticed that someone was following me. From what I could tell, it was Officer Sean. No doubt he thought he was tailing Nicole.

I drove to the nearest service centre, and as I got out of the car, I turned and waved to Sean, smirking at his look of surprise and anger. He peeled away in a huff.

This time I bought two tires instead of one since I had little doubt that I'd need another at some point, and then I headed over to Leonardo's. I walked into the pizza place cautiously. He looked up with a bright smile that quickly turned into a frown when he saw me. "Mr. Leonardo, how are you today? By any chance, can I order a pizza?" I smiled sweetly.

"No pizza. You have news for me?"

I filled him in with what I'd learned so far, all the while cognizant of the fact that he, too, had a strong motive for killing Alphie. Which was of course why I was there. Wrapping up my summary, and not wanting to alienate him after all the progress we'd made in our relationship, I said, "What I find hard to believe, since you're such a successful and respected businessman, is that some people say that even you owed Alphie money."

His back stiffened and his eyes blazed but he quickly regained his composure, realizing that I wasn't accusing him but passing on the information I'd learned. I had taken great care when choosing my words so as not to offend him and destroy the thread of friendship that had started. Okay, perhaps friendship was an exaggeration.

He sighed. "Bah! I hate him, yes, but it's true that I borrow money from him." He then proceeded to tell me that some of his kitchen equipment had broken down several years ago and money had been tight. He'd been approved at the bank for a loan but Alphie had convinced him that he'd give him a special rate. Instead, he'd demanded a never-ending payback.

Leonardo was used to having to keep meticulous records of everything, having been in business for twenty-five years, and he was certain that he'd more than paid back the loan, but Alphie kept insisting that he owed more. As he spoke, his cheeks flushed with anger. At some point, he'd picked up a block of mozzarella and was now pounding the cheese on the counter as he spoke.

Having been on the receiving end of his temper many times, I knew firsthand how volatile he could be. I had no trouble believing that he may have killed Alphie. Stashing him in my garage would have been a bonus in his eyes because of his strong dislike of me at the time. Who are we kidding? He still disliked me, but he was being tolerant. The question was, why? Suddenly, he moved to the top of my suspect list.

"I'm sorry to hear that. Did you often see Alphie? I mean, I know he worked right next door to you practically, but would he come in here often or go over to your house?"

"Every day he come here and ask for lunch. He never pay. He say I owe him!"

I thanked him and left, going a couple of doors down to the Dollar Store. I needed a few odds and ends and hadn't been in there yet. I was in the kitchen gadget aisle when I heard a familiar laugh one aisle over. My ears perked up when I heard a male voice responding to Chloé.

"Do you really have to work tonight? Man, she was such a bitch yesterday, I don't know how you can stand her! Why don't you call in sick?" Jeff said.

"Yes, I do have to work, I need the extra money and she's not a bitch. You were there the night of the murder so she was just worried about me," she replied, her tone icy. I was happy to hear her stand up for me.

"Yeah, I guess so," he replied sullenly. They moved out of ear shot. By the time I got to the cash, they were nowhere to be seen and having had enough excitement for one day, I headed back home. In the bistro kitchen, I gave my hot dish, Cheesy Potatoes, a quick stir, plucked out a piece of bacon for a taste-test then placed the lid back on the slow cooker. Suddenly drained, I looked at the clock and was happy to see that I had a bit of time for a quick nap.

CHRIS'S CHEESY POTATOES

I don't take credit for this recipe but I do make them differently than my friend Chris. She uses full-fat ingredients whereas I, being an ex-anorexic, always use a lower fat version.

You need a slow cooker for this (easiest) however I'm told you can bake all this in an oven for about an hour (half hour covered, half hour uncovered).

- 16 good sized potatoes, peeled and cubed
- 2 cans cream of cheddar soup
- ½ cup diced onions
- Garlic (a couple of minced cloves or cheat and use garlic powder)
- 2 teaspoons parsley (I just use dried)
- 1 teaspoon dried dill weed (not the seed, the green part)
- ½ cup mayonnaise (I use light)
- 1 cup sour cream (light) or plain yogurt or Greek yogurt
- 1 package of cooked and chopped bacon- not super crispy but definitely already cooked

- A little shake from a jar of paprika
- Salt and pepper, if needed (taste after 6 hours before you decide)

Dump all of the above into a slow cooker and cook on low until potatoes are tender (varies by slow cooker, could be 6-8 hours, maybe even longer). Stir from time to time and taste after 6 hours. If it's getting too thick, add a bit of milk or even water.

CHAPTER SEVENTEEN

On Monday I was totally exhausted and spent most of the day lazing around. Nora had officially broken up with Leonardo the night before, Nicole had slept over at Chloé's place and Matt had returned to his home after replacing my slashed tire. After a long sleep, I went into town for some errands then returned home for more sleep. Before I knew it, it was Tuesday night.

Alas! Pole dancing night.

My parents lured me to their place for dinner with a promise of schnitzel. Although I refuse to fry food at home, I do indulge guilt free whenever my mom makes it. As I walked into the house I could hear the welcoming sizzle of frying meat and my mouth watered. I set the table and then looked around to see that every last box had been unpacked. I noted more framed cross stitch pictures on the walls and shuddered.

After dinner, my mom changed into her "exercise" clothes. One must understand that my mom doesn't exercise. She's always puttering about and doing things around the house, but in terms of actual exercise, like walking or sit-ups or anything like that, never to my knowledge.

She modelled her thick, red sweat pants that she had

149

paired with her red and black "do you think I'm Sexy" top that was a Whine and Cheese promotional t-shirt she'd gotten from me when she'd recently helped me at the bistro. I couldn't complain; at least this time she matched. Last time she wore the shirt, she had paired it with yellow sweats.

We headed to the community center and said hello to the others that were there for the pole dancing. My lips twitched as I noted the curious stares that my mother was getting. We were both the oldest in the class.

"What made you change your mind about pole dancing?" I couldn't resist asking my mom.

She shrugged. "It gets me out of the house. Papa drives me crazy sometimes."

Just then our instructor arrived and told us each to choose a pole. There were a dozen of them scattered about, bolted to the ceiling and the floor.

"Today we're going to learn three moves. The Fireman, Pinwheel and the V-spin," she announced in a perky voice, while twirling around her pole and flaunting her perfectly lean body. I took a fairly instant dislike to her.

We watched her demonstrate the Fireman. "Stretch your dominant arm as high as possible and grab the pole. Now, stand on the tips of your toes and take three steps around the pole." This part was easy. "On the fourth step, keeping your weight away from the pole, lift your opposite arm then grab the pole at about shoulder length. Straddle your ankles around the pole as you go into your spin. Lower your body as you spin then raise your body as you continue to spin."

She made it look so easy and the twenty-something year olds had no problems spinning about flawlessly. Neither my mother nor I looked particularly graceful, but with fifteen minutes' practice, I had to admit we didn't look horrible either. I peeked at my mom and caught her grinning at me. "Better than polka!" she whispered to me in English.

Next came the Pinwheel, and then finally the dreaded V-spin.

"Now, as you spin, lift both legs off the ground and hold them straight in front of you with your crotch facing the pole, then, as you support your weight with both arms, spin," she said as she demonstrated. My poor mom landed hard on her butt and let out a loud grunt. The instructor smiled kindly. "Nice try, Mrs. Kis. Now let me see you try it again."

Five grunts and a *bazd meg* later, the class was thankfully over and my mom was rubbing her tushy vigorously. "Papa, he gonna thinking you beat me," she joked.

I smiled. I'd had fun with my mom, having never seen such a playful side of her personality. I was already looking forward to the next class when she admitted that she wasn't sure if she'd come the following week, and said she'd wait to see how much bruising she had from the first class. But I was pleased to see a blush in her cheeks and I could tell that she'd enjoyed it.

Matt came by around nine that evening after verifying that Nicole had returned to my house. We gathered in the living room with a glass of Sexy, inspired by my mom's t-shirt. He leered at me as he asked about the pole dancing class.

"Maybe I'll demonstrate one day," I joked before we got down to the business at hand.

"Nicole, any more contact from Sean?"

She barked with laughter in response. "Countless messages and texts; see for yourself." She handed her phone to Matt for review. I watched as his mouth grew thinner by the minute. He looked at us with steel in his eyes.

"Alright, it's time for action." Matt outlined his plan for us. "Nicole, are you comfortable with setting up a meeting with him tomorrow night, at your place? I spoke to a buddy of mine who's still on the force, as I promised you I would. If I can have the keys to your place, we'll go and hook up some cameras and audio equipment and then we'll monitor from the next room. Once we have it all captured on film, we'll come out and have a friendly little man to man chat with him. If he ever stalks you again, we'll be sure to turn the evidence over to his boss. I have a feeling that just the threat of it will be enough to make him come to his senses. We'll insist he seek help, of course, something like anger management. He's a good cop, though, or at least he used to be, so I'd like to give him a chance."

Nicole readily agreed and texted Sean, not wanting to have to actually speak to him.

How about coming over tomorrow night around seven, and we can talk about things?

The return message was almost instant.

Sure, I'll bring dinner.

"It's all set," she confirmed as she handed Matt her key. I walked him to his car so that I could have a moment alone with him.

"It's really nice of you to help out like this. Nicole doesn't have family close by, and I know it means a lot to her to have your help." I gave him a gentle kiss. Our bodies were flush against each other and I could feel the heat.

"When this is all over, maybe you can spend a few nights at my place," he said.

His suggestion could not have been more welcome.

Ah, you were expecting a recipe! Remember, this isn't a recipe book, although I have shared some of my favorites with you. You can skip a couple of chapters if you're really anxious for details on how to make my tasty Bavarian Apple Torte. Otherwise, keep reading to see how things turned out with Officer Sean.

CHAPTER EIGHTEEN

Everyone had already left early for work at their regular jobs and Matt was busy preparing the items he would need to later set things up at Nicole's apartment. Yet again, I was awake early and climbing the walls, feeling excited and nervous about what would happen at Nicole's place.

I was also feeling frustrated that nothing was happening with regards to solving the murder, and I was feeling a little guilty because I hadn't yet gotten around to talking to Matt about Billy. I was still struggling with the decision to get involved or not, and to what extent.

I paced around trying to burn energy (and a little weight). One cannot stay naturally slim when wine and cheese are the staples in their diet, especially if one has an uncooperative thyroid. I danced around a little and found myself idly wishing that I had a pole to practice with, and then snickered as I imagined the bistro with poles. As I pranced about, giggling, my eyes fell upon the photocopy of the reservation page from the night of the murder and a name jumped out at me: Jeff. Chloé's new beau and part of the ski-do crowd. He had booked a table for a party of twelve that night. I stopped mid-boogie, staring at his name and came up with a plan.

Other than my slashed tires, things were too quiet. Everyone seemed to be lying low, as if waiting for it to all blow over. It was time to stir things up a bit. I didn't like this nasty crime hanging over the bistro like a dark shadow, and I didn't like the notion that the murderer might be hanging out at the bistro. That thought made my arm hairs stand on end.

I whipped out my little laptop and did a reverse phone number search. Luck was on my side as his number was listed and I was able to get his address. I jotted it down then typed up a simple note, written in eighteen-inch Copperplate Gothic Bold font, which I thought looked appropriately menacing:

I KNOW WHAT YOU DID

Okay, so maybe it was a stupid plan, but it was the only plan I had. I changed out of my PJs in a flash and jammed my hair into a ponytail then rushed out the door.

I drove quickly to the farthest house on my list and slithered up the walkway in the dark, taping a note to Cathy and Markus's door. I imagined myself scurrying about like the Grinch when he's stealing the presents and Christmas trees from Who Ville and had to stifle my giggles.

I zipped back to the town of Robin and did the same at Valerie's house and then Jeff's, who lived just a couple of minutes away from her. Next, I visited the strip mall, taping one on the door of Leonardo's pizza place and one on the door of the post office. (Even if Leonardo was innocent, he still deserved it for being so crabby, and for sleeping with Nora.) For good measure, I also posted one on the door at each of the other businesses at the strip mall: the grocery store, dollar store, liquor store and the chiropractic office. I figured that quite possibly any of these places may have been involved in shady dealings with Alphie and that I just hadn't unearthed it yet. It was a good place to start, albeit quite likely a wild goose chase. I had nothing to lose. If they were innocent, then they would just think the note was a prank and no harm was done.

It was still early, not even eight in the morning by the time I was done, so none of the businesses were open yet. I hadn't come across a single person, and as I glanced about, I was relieved not to see a single surveillance camera. This was a small town, after all, and we generally didn't need big city gadgets, even if we were part of greater Ottawa.

I returned to the bistro, drank coffee and watched my cooking shows until about ten o'clock when I started to get antsy again and couldn't concentrate. Each recipient should have seen his note by now, and I peered outside anxiously, scanning the area for approaching cars. Nothing yet.

I put on makeup and styled my hair then did a load of laundry, followed by some pacing. Then I cleaned the kitchen counters and noticed a cabinet with a loose screw so I tightened it. Acting on impulse, I slipped the screwdriver into my hoodie pocket. It was a short handled one and would make a fine weapon if needed. I was growing more nervous by the second, and if nothing else, it might come in handy later that night when Officer Sean was being confronted and we "put the screws" to him. Again, I laughed to myself.

It was the end of January and it was an uncharacteristically warm day, almost fooling me into believing spring was near. Hummer, too, looked longingly outside and stared in fascination as the water dripped from the icicles that were hanging precariously from the eaves. The warmth was calling to me; if nothing happened soon, I decided I would go for a hike.

Having run out of things to do, I went down to the bistro and puttered about there, continuing with my cleaning frenzy and constantly looking out the window, convinced that my note would trigger a reaction. By two o'clock, I finally decided that nothing would likely happen until the work day was over. At this point, if anyone suspected that the note had come from me, then I'd probably only see them under cover of night.

It now occurred to me that the culprit might never suspect that I was the writer of the note, or that none of the people addressed were even involved in Alphie's murder. I had to think of something clever, and fresh air would clear my mind.

I packed a treat bag, intending to find Billy on the trails and added a Ziploc bag of full of Cheerios for Chicha. I set out for my hike, enjoying the feel of the sun on my face. It had been a long winter and I had lived in Ottawa long enough to know that it wasn't over yet. Although it was warm, the temperature would again fall below zero soon.

I hiked the trail all the way to Joey's house with no sign of Billy. On the trek back, I left his goodie bag near where Matt and I had seen his tent. Hopefully he would find the bag.

I put Chicha's Cheerios into my coat pocket and continued my hike back slowly, enjoying every moment of the sun. It reminded me of a line from a dark poem I had written in my teens:

Sunshine. The fatalistic foreshadowing of false pretenses.

Suddenly, I shivered, having thoroughly succeeded in creeping myself out.

I joined Chicha in the garage and she grunted as she gnashed her treat. I put the leash on her and coerced her outside. "Come on, Chicha. Try to poop outside instead of in my garage!"

Finally getting her out, we stood there behind the garage. I looked at her expectantly. She blinked. She didn't seem to want to do much. "Fine, we'll just stand here in the sun until you do your business," I told her. I felt a drip on my head and looked up to see a thick icicle hanging precariously above me, only inches away.

And that's when I figured it out.

CHAPTER NINETEEN

*"B*rilliant!" I exclaimed. "Absolutely brilliant! No wonder they couldn't figure out the murder weapon or find any trace of it. It had melted!" I explained excitedly to Chicha. Seeing the size of this one, I had no doubt that whoever had killed Alphie had done so by driving one of these massive icicles through his eye and piercing his brain. That's what my subconscious had been trying to tell me when I was drinking the ice wine. Inniskillin—kill; and ice wine—ice. Kill and ice!

Chicha was less than excited by my revelation.

But I was mentally high-fiving myself when I heard the sound of feet crunching on snow. I whirled around and, admittedly, was surprised to see who was standing there, not looking very friendly.

I had known there was a chance. After all, the spouse is always one of the first suspects, but in all honestly, I figured she would have been the least likely to show up today. I was wrong. "Hello, Valerie." I said calmly. She walked slowly toward me as I moved slowly away. "May I help you?" I said. She didn't speak as she continued to approach. I was now backed up against the pig. She was about four feet away from me. I put my hands inside my hoodie, pretending to keep them warm. She didn't look armed, but then again, neither did I, but I had my trusty screwdriver.

"How did you find out?" she demanded, getting straight to the point.

I played dumb. "What do you mean? Find out what? Do you mean how did I find Alphie that day?"

She yanked the note I'd written out of her coat pocket and held it up. I continued to play dumb as I squinted at it as though I'd never seen it before. I wanted to flush out the killer, but I certainly wasn't in any position to take them down by myself. I just wanted to know who it was then hand them over to the cops.

"I have no clue what you mean, but you look quite upset. Let's go inside and talk and have a glass of wine?" I suggested, while keeping a close eye on the massive dangling icicle. If she made one move toward it, I would tackle her.

"I don't want to talk. Here. Just take this," she said, shoving two hundred dollar bills in my direction. I was utterly confused.

"Are you trying to pay me off?" I stammered. "If you are, then it will take a lot more than two hundred bucks!"

"It's just a slashed tire, for heaven's sake. Don't be greedy. I'm sure a new tire costs less than that," she snapped at me.

The tire? "It was two tires—winter tires at that," I huffed in return

"Two? Then I guess you pissed someone else off, too. I only slashed one." She threw the money on the ground then started to walk away.

"Wait!" I yelled. "Why did I piss you off? I'm only trying to figure out who killed your husband. I'm trying to help you."

"Maybe I don't care who killed him. He wasn't exactly a saint, you know." She stomped away.

I pushed and prodded Chicha back into the garage. With my nerves jangled, I thought I caught a glimmer of movement out of the corner of my eye, but before I could focus, all went still. Feeling as though I were being watched, I hurried back inside. Valerie might not have been the killer, but that didn't mean the killer wasn't close by.

I changed out of my sweaty clothes, put on a fresh hoodie and transferred my screwdriver into the pocket. For some reason, having it there gave me a sense of safety. I grabbed a quick bite to eat and headed over to Nicole's place.

"She's not here yet," Matt informed me, as he opened the door. I grinned and took advantage of the moment, wrapping my arms around him and giving him a passionate kiss.

"We're on camera," he whispered into my ear.

"Oops," I grinned sheepishly. We then went into Nicole's bedroom, where Ricky was waiting and smirking at us. To my surprise, Nora was already there, waiting for the show to begin. She, too, was smirking and gave me a thumbs-up.

I debated whether or not to tell them about the note I'd written and about Valerie showing up at my house and admitting to having slashed one of my tires. I even opened my mouth and was about to blurt it out, then decided against it. I didn't want Matt lecturing me, or to distract him from the task at hand.

Before I could change my mind, Nicole arrived and then we all waited impatiently for Sean. She paced nervously while we assured her that nothing would go wrong. Just before seven, there was a knock at her door and Matt and Ricky sprang to life, positioning themselves in front of the monitoring devices and indicating for us to remain quiet. Closing the bedroom door behind her, we watched Nicole on the monitor as she answered Sean's knock.

He swaggered in then immediately turned into an octopus, arms all over the place, trying to hug her and grab her. "Stop it!" she said sharply. "We need to talk, and you need to keep your hands to yourself!" Surprisingly, he listened to her and placed some take-out bags of Chinese food on her dining table.

"Sure, Baby. Come over here and sit with me." He indicated his lap but she sat on one of her dining room chairs, a safe distance away.

"Why do you keep calling me and texting me when I've asked you to stop?" She got right to the point, eager to have it out. "Surely you should have your hands full with the murder at Amalia's place and chasing down leads. I don't understand how you have time to stalk me."

He looked surprised. "It's driving me crazy, thinking you're with someone else, or that I have lost you. I know I messed up, but you have to give me another chance. Let's just relax and have dinner and start all over," he pleaded. This was nothing like the cool and distant Officer Sean with whom the rest of us were familiar.

"Sean, listen to me. It's over, and I want you to lose my number and forget about me. No more calls, no more texts, or I'll have to report you to your boss. Do you really want that to happen?"

His eyes narrowed. "What did I ever do to you? Anyway, we cops look out for each other, and you'd be sorry if you..." He got up from the couch and moved toward her. "Come on now, enough playing hard to get. Let me show you how much I miss you."

She jumped up from her chair and put her hand out in front of her. "Stay right where you are! I don't want you to take another step towards me. It's over and I don't want to see you again. Do you understand?"

He lunged toward her as fast as a cheetah. Just as quickly, Matt and Ricky shot out of the bedroom. Nora and I exchanged a glance then hurried out after them.

"Step back, Sean," Matt ordered as Sean froze in surprise. "We've got you on tape, and we have a copy of all the texts and voicemails that you left Nicole. If you ever, even once, contact her again, Ricky and I will go to the Chief and turn over the evidence. Do you really want to risk your job? And while we're at it, if I catch wind of you stalking anyone else, just remember, we've got the tapes. Consider yourself warned."

His face red and angry, Sean swore like a sailor. "Perfect, Sean; that's a great finale. The tape is still running. I think we caught your good side in a few shots." Ricky said. He had never liked Sean and wasted no effort trying to hide his feelings. "This is our final warning. Don't be an idiot and throw away your career. Now get out and stay away from Nicole."

Sean stood, with his fists balled up at his sides, panting with the exertion of keeping his temper in check. Then he grabbed his bags of Chinese food and stormed to the door. Just before he left, he turned, gave a last menacing glance at Nicole, threw one of the bags of food down to the floor then slammed the door forcefully on his way out.

We all stared mutely at the mess on the floor. Some of the containers of food had burst open and spilled out of the bag, and there in the midst of the mess was a gold ring with a single diamond winking at us.

Nicole backed away in horror and collapsed onto the chair she'd been sitting on earlier. She looked pale. "My God, I think I wet myself," she squeaked. Her hands were shaking and I rushed into her bedroom, grabbed the quilt off her bed and brought it over to her.

"It's over Nicole. If he dares to do anything again, we've got everything on video, and you can press charges. I don't think he'll be that stupid though."

Just to be on the safe side, we insisted she return to my place for the next few nights while Matt or Ricky would alternate staying at her place to keep watch and make sure that Sean didn't return. Matt walked with us to my car and as we approached, he swore.

"Damn it! Again?" I exclaimed. Another tire slashed, and one of the new ones at that! "But I just happen to have an extra in the trunk, if you wouldn't mind changing it for me?" I smiled sweetly and batted my eyelashes at Matt.

"Open the trunk," he replied sullenly. "I'm going to have to pay Sean a little visit, I think. There's no doubt in my mind that it was him this time, and that it's not a coincidence. I wonder if he slashed the others, too. Maybe he wanted to scare you off to prevent you from snooping," he wondered aloud. I kept quiet, not wanting to blurt out my news about Valerie in the parking lot.

"Matt, do you think Sean could have anything to do with the murder?" I picked at the hunch that I'd had a little while ago, exploring it out loud now. "I know it's a reach, but he certainly hasn't done much about finding the murderer."

"I don't see it, Mali. Sure, he's off his crate, but I don't see why he'd have any reason to kill Alphie. If it makes you feel any better, I'll poke around a bit to see if he owed him money or something, but you stay out of it. I almost lost you once, and I don't want you in danger." He gave me a soft kiss then set to work changing my tire. When he had finished, he said, "All right, we're done here. I'm glad it's not minus twenty today. I'm going inside to help Ricky dismantle the equipment then I'll swing by your place a bit later to make sure everything's okay. You gals stick together. Where's Nora?"

"She left a few minutes before we did. We'll make sure we stick together," I promised.

We hurried home but Nora's car was nowhere in sight. I was about to send her a text when I saw that she'd already sent one to me.

I had a message from Leo, so I've gone to see him. I'll be home soon.

I pictured the hair on his back and shuddered.

CHAPTER TWENTY

Nicole was still shivering when we settled on the couch. "I can't believe he had a ring for me," she said, stunned.

I didn't know how to respond so I just blurted out what came naturally. "Wine?"

She nodded. "Do you still have any of that ice wine?"

"Yes. I'll just go down to the bistro for a bottle. Why don't you take a nice hot shower or bath in the meantime?"

I went downstairs via my secret stairway and retrieved the ice wine from the fridge. I glanced into the dining area out of habit and a flash of light coming from the parking lot caught my eye. I quickly crossed the room to peek out the blinds. A car was parked there, its headlights directed at the bistro, the driver making no move to get out. With the headlights directly in my eyes, I couldn't make out much. Maybe it was Matt. Or maybe that scoundrel, Hans. My eyes narrowed. I thought I could almost make out his big blonde head bobbing as he laughed at me. Before I could stop myself, curiosity and rage got the better of me and I flung open the front door and headed toward the car. The driver looked at me in surprise then lowered his window. It was not Hans. "Sorry Ma'am, I didn't mean to alarm you. I'm just trying to find a street," he apologized, and I could see he was holding a map. "Do you know where I will find Second Line Road?"

I gave him directions and he apologized again. It wasn't uncommon for cars to turn around in my driveway when they discovered that they were lost. It didn't usually occur to them that someone lived here. Relieved, I went back inside and locked the door, double checking each bolt and taking a final peek out the blinds. All was quiet now. I turned to head back upstairs and froze.

There wasn't a sound, nor was anything out of place, only a smell. Cologne, or perhaps perfume. I walked slowly to the table where I'd put down the bottle of Inniskillin and picked it up as casually as I could, humming a little la-dee-da tune while trying to act normal. I had left the bistro dining area in the dark when I had gone outside, but the kitchen was still lit. I made my way toward it now, hoping I was wrong, my ears at attention for the slightest sound, my eyes searching for the slightest movement. Halfway through the room, my hackles rose so I went with my instinct and whirled around then ran to the front door, throwing open the bolts and running outside. Somehow, I thought I'd be safer if I wasn't in a confined space. I was barely a foot out the door when I was tackled to the ground, falling face first into the partially melted snow and losing my grip on the bottle of ice wine. It didn't break, but rolled just out of reach.

The person remained on my back, roughly grabbing my hair close to the roots and then smashing my face into the ground again. I felt searing pain and then a wave of blackness tried to grip me, but I knew I couldn't succumb to it. Ignoring the pain in my face as best as I could, I bucked with all my strength and managed to throw the person off me. I rolled over in time to see the figure lunging toward me again. I raised a leg and connected with the stomach as the person tried to jump on me. The assailant staggered, falling to the ground, as I struggled to my feet, fighting the fear and nausea and gagging from the blood running down the back of my throat. I threw a kick, aiming at the head, but the person recovered quicker than I'd hoped and grabbed my leg, pulling it out from under me. I landed hard on my left elbow and yelped out in pain. "Why are you doing this?" I yelled, hoping to stall for time and to find out who it was as I hadn't been able to catch a good glimpse at the face yet.

"You just won't stop, will you? Why do you have to keep poking into things?" She stood and took a few determined steps toward my house. With horror, I watched her reach up and grab a giant hanging icicle, much like the one that I had discovered hanging from my garage. The temperature had fallen several degrees since then, however, so this one would likely be solid. Then, before I could make it back onto my feet, she rushed toward me and swung it like a bat, catching me on the side of the ear and grazing my cheek as I rolled away just in time. I remembered my screwdriver, but her weapon was longer than mine. I'd have to get closer.

She stood there panting and I withdrew the screwdriver from my pocket. She squinted to see what I was holding, unsure because of the lack of light. I took advantage of the moment and sprung to my feet, almost passing out as the blood rushed from my head. Her eyes were locked on what was in my hand and then she started laughing as the shape of it registered. She swung at me again.

I faked right but, since my legs had not yet healed and were still sore, I fumbled when I faked to the left and I managed to trip myself. She lunged forward and brought the icicle down full force. I shifted as much as I could in my weakened state and awkward position, but it was no good, she got me. The icicle pierced the fleshy part of my thigh through my thin yoga pants and I screamed out in pain and fury. Any man would have been proud of the swear words I let loose.

169

"Ooops, I missed. I was aiming for your face. Let me fix that," she said, sweet as pie, and then approached the house, looking for more icicles. I tried to stagger to my feet, but she was too quick and was already heading toward me.

As she approached, with every last ounce of my strength, I thrust myself forward, managing to grab her around her knees and knocking her down. I tried to jab at her with the screwdriver but she was dressed in full ski-do style snowsuit gear and it was too thick to pierce. I could see the icicle approaching my face, as promised, and I rolled away just in time.

She lurched to her feet and was above me in a split second, glaring down at me. Suddenly, she was knocked out of the way and stumbled but quickly regained her balance, whirled toward me again, hesitated, then ran out of the parking lot and disappeared down the street.

I looked up, struggling to focus through the tears in my eyes then breathed a deep sigh of relief. Billy!

Then I lost consciousness.

CHAPTER TWENTY-ONE

I don't know how long I was unconscious but when I came to I was inside the bistro, laid out on one of my couches. My leg was wrapped tightly in something, and from what I could discern, the icicle was no longer inside me. There was a glass of water and what appeared to be Tylenol on one of the small bistro tables next to me. Billy was nowhere to be seen.

I was reaching for the pills when I heard Nicole calling for me. "Over here. Down in the bistro, on one of the couches," I yelled back hoarsely. Shakily, I leaned back onto the couch.

"Did you start without me? Sorry I took such a long bath, but you were right, it was a great idea. I feel much better now. I still can't believe he was going to give me a ring. I wonder, was he going to propose? Why are you in the dark?" She switched on the light and headed toward me. Suddenly, she stopped. "Mali? What did you do to yourself?" She was looking at my face and hadn't even noticed my bandaged leg yet. Then her gaze fell and she froze completely. "What in the world happened?"

"Not sure," I replied with a dry throat. "May have been

Nancy. Or Valerie. Or someone else entirely. She was wearing full ski-do gear and a baklava on her face, so I couldn't really tell." She looked at me blankly.

"Baklava? On her face? Why? How? Uh, do you mean a balaclava, like a ski mask?" I nodded. "How did she get in and what did she do to you?"

"I went outside to speak to someone who was sitting in a car and looking for directions. I'm not sure now if that was real or if it was staged. She must have gotten into the bistro then. I sensed something was wrong and ran back outside, but she tackled me, groomed the snow with my face a couple of times and then stabbed me with an icicle. Which, by the way, I'm pretty sure was the murder weapon that killed Alphie, so my guess is that this person was also involved in killing him."

She listened, her eyes widening in horror and with a hand covering her mouth. "How come she didn't kill you? I mean, I'm glad she didn't, but how did you get away? And what happened after that?"

"Billy, the guy who's been living in the forest along the trails, showed up. He shoved her out of the way, then I guess she figured she couldn't take us both on and bolted. He must have bandaged me up and then disappeared again, figuring that "they" would catch him if he stuck around."

"They? The killer's after him too?" Nicole asked in surprise. I hadn't thought of that.

"I don't think so. I think "they" are in his head, but I wonder if the killer might be after him too. If he or she knows about him, they might think he saw something and he could be in real danger. Help me get upstairs; we need to call Matt. And the cops, too, I guess."

She blanched, no doubt picturing Officer Sean showing up on the scene. "Don't worry, I don't think Sean is on duty tonight. He wasn't in uniform at your place, right?" She nodded.

"Oh wait! The ice-wine. It's outside." I started toward

the door but she stopped me, glaring. "I'll get it; you just wait." She was back in a moment, holding up the ice-wine and a screwdriver, looking confused.

"That's mine; it didn't do any good. I couldn't pierce her snow suit with it." I hobbled to the kitchen and put it in my junk drawer, the false sense of safety it gave me now gone.

Back upstairs, Nicole poured the wine and fixed a plate of cheese. Delicious Gouda, a little wedge of brie, a wedge of Irish Cheddar and a couple of rounds of goat cheese. She spread some of the goat cheese on a piece of baguette and handed it to me, the concern clear on her face.

"I'm fine," I insisted, but accepted the food gratefully. "Let me call Matt to make sure he still plans to come over." I dialed and it went straight to voicemail, but at the same time, my doorbell rang. Nicole rushed to get it and sighed in relief as she threw open the door. "It's him."

"Him? Were you ladies just gossiping about me?" Matt joked and smiled before his features froze as his gaze fell upon my face. In all the excitement about my leg, I had forgotten that my face had been injured. He asked a single question: "Do we need backup?" I nodded yes. He was on the phone immediately.

"Ricky, change of plans. I need you here tonight on guard outside. Get over here as soon as you can. No, I don't know what's going on yet, but Amalia looks like she's been worked over." By the time he hung up, he was by my side, his free hand holding mine. I saw him swallow hard before he spoke to me. "Are you okay?" he asked softly. I nodded and a tear made a little wet path down my cheek. Until now, I hadn't had a chance to feel sorry for myself, but his gentle voice was my undoing. He held me, stroking my hair and rocking me slightly. When my sniffles subsided, Nicole handed me the Kleenex box and then gave Matt the information that I'd already told her, sparing me the effort. I watched as his features grew bleaker by the minute. When she mentioned my theory about the icicle as the murder weapon, he got the same "aha" look in his eyes that I'd had. "But why did this person come after you now?" he wondered out loud. "It doesn't make sense." His eyes bore into me and I couldn't hold his look. "Amalia? Anything else?"

I nodded guiltily. "I might have written a little note and left it at all the known suspects' houses this morning." Was it only this morning? So much had happened since then. "All I wrote was that I knew what they had done. I figured that if any of them were guilty, then it might spark some action, but I didn't really think they'd come after me. It's not like I signed my name to it or anything. I did expect maybe someone to stop by for a chat and try to get some information out of me, but I didn't expect an attack." Matt groaned and tore at his hair in frustration. I dabbed at my eyes again and then continued. "Valerie had stopped by this afternoon and gave me two hundred dollars. It turns out that she'd slashed one of my tires and thought the note was about that. She also said that she didn't care that Alphie was dead, but I don't think she's the one that killed him."

"So, Billy patched you up but didn't stick around, is that right? Did you call the cops yet? And then we better get you to the hospital to get your wounds properly looked after." He went to the kitchen and came back with a wet dishcloth. He sat down next to me again and dabbed gently at my nose. I winced and he stopped for a moment, then dabbed again, commenting on the dried blood and mumbling something about hoping that my nose wasn't broken. He called the cops for me and we waited, morosely nibbling on cheese and drinking the ice wine. "Ironic, isn't it?" he said, nodding towards the bottle of Inniskillin.

I nodded. "It struck me a while back, but I couldn't figure out what my subconscious was trying to tell me at the time. When Chicha and I figured it out earlier today, I was pretty excited. You should have seen the size of the icicles, Matt. I'm sure it was the murder weapon. Look, it was thick and sharp enough to pierce my skin. An eyeball would have been no problem. It must have been like stabbing through fresh snow."

We were saved from that mental image by the arrival of the police. Luckily, Officer Sean was not among them. I recounted the pertinent events of the day while an officer took my statement and someone else snapped photos.

"So let me get this straight, she was waiting for you inside, but when she attacked you outside, she was armed only with an icicle? What would she have done if you'd stayed inside?"

I hadn't thought of that. I shrugged.

"Alright, I've got an officer checking downstairs, and then we'll look around outside. I don't suppose you have any security cameras?" I shook my head. "You keeping watch on her?" he asked Matt, with whom he was already familiar.

"She's my girlfriend," he said as he took a moment to smile tenderly at me. "I've got a guy who'll be stationed outside tonight".

The cop went off to help his partner with the search and returned about thirty minutes later, holding up a hunting knife in a baggie. "This yours?" he asked.

"I've never seen it," I replied. "Where was it?"

"Behind the bar. She must have dropped it when she came after you. Maybe we'll get lucky and get her prints."

"I doubt it, Officer; she was wearing gloves," I replied.

They packed up their equipment and then Matt helped me into his car. He went over to where Ricky was parked, on the look-out, and they spoke for a few minutes before he joined me again. "Ricky's going to keep watch here for the night. Where is Nora's car?"

"She went to Leo's. I guess she still hasn't returned. I'll text her so that she doesn't get spooked by Ricky's car in the lot if she comes back tonight."

"I thought they broke up?" Matt said.

175

"I thought they did too," I said.

"Any chance he's the killer?" Matt asked me.

"I think it's very slim, and he doesn't even know that Nora and I know each other, so I don't think she'd be in danger," I replied. Unless, of course, he'd followed her at some point, but that seemed unlikely.

After a few hours wait at the hospital, my leg received three stitches and my face was X-rayed for fractures. The good news was that my nose wasn't broken. The bad news was that the bruising would likely be just as bad as if I had broken it. They took a look at the elbow that I'd fallen on but I already knew that that wasn't broken either, just incredibly sore. They gave me a lovely injection for all my pain and suffering and told me to take Tylenol for the next few days. With the amount of Tylenol I'd been taking the past few weeks, I started to seriously think about buying it in bulk.

Back home, Matt gently tucked me into my bed and informed me he'd be on the couch. I heard the outer door open and close, though, and suspected he was going out to speak with Ricky and to check the area himself. I fell into a gloriously deep and long sleep. When I awoke, I wished that I'd had some of that lovely medicine that they'd pumped into me at the hospital. Everything was throbbing. I tried to remember what day it was. Thursday, I thought. Damn, the bistro would be open that night. I'd have to stay in the kitchen to avoid being the target of the local gossip mill.

I limped into the living room and smiled at the sight of Matt's feet that were hanging off the couch. Hummer was sitting under them, craning his neck for a sniff, and then stretching his tongue out to lick them. Matt's foot jerked and he sat up on the couch in alarm. "What was that?" he asked groggily.

"Just Hummer snacking on your toes. I'll make coffee if you're awake now?" He nodded as he put his head back on the pillow. My hero...

Once the coffee had perked I brought him a steaming mugful, nudging him awake. He gratefully took a long swallow then frowned as he looked at my face and the bruises already forming. I shrugged. Neither of us knew what to say so we drank in silence for a while.

Energized by the coffee, Matt called the officer who had been there the previous night to see if he had any new information. The police had spoken with Valerie, Nancy and Cathy, but only Cathy had an alibi as her husband confirmed she'd been home the entire evening. The other two ladies, being single, had no one to vouch for them, but neither broke down and confessed. Neither admitted to having ski-do type snowsuits and both refused to let officers look around without a search warrant in hand. Progress, once again, was at a standstill.

"What now?" I asked Matt. "My note seemed to get a reaction, but now the killer will be lying low again, and I don't know which woman attacked me. This is frustrating."

"We need to let the cops do their job," Matt replied firmly, pinning me with a look. "Didn't last night tell you something?"

"Yes, it told me that I have to sign up for a self-defense class," I snapped at him. "It's got to be one of those women. They all slept with Alphie at some point, so they're all connected somehow, and how else would that woman last night have known to grab the icicle to attack me?" I saw something flicker in his eyes. "What? What did I say?"

"Maybe they are somehow connected. Do we know if they're friends or related or anything? Maybe it's not just one killer. Maybe they've banded together for some reason? And if that's the case, what we're dealing with here would be all the more dangerous."

"Valerie and Nancy did seem to be friendly," I mentioned. "Valerie and Cathy, however, did not. Cathy seemed pretty angry at her, in fact."

"What about Nancy and Cathy?" he suggested. I shrugged. "Well, that's what we need to find out then. Let's go," he said, then paused, taking in my pajamas. He'd slept fully clothed so he was ready to go.

"I thought you wanted me to stay out of this?" I reminded him.

"I do. I'll handle it. I thought I'd like to see her reaction though when she sees your lovely, banged-up face."

I put on some fresh yoga pants, lamenting that my old ones were now ruined. Oh sure, I suppose I could have sewn them, if I knew how to sew, however that was not one of my talents. Drinking wine, that was a true talent!

I finished getting dressed before facing The Mirror. So far, I'd avoided looking at myself, but the time was here. I took a deep breath, turned on the light in the bathroom and faced myself. It was not a pretty sight. Both eyes looked blackened and my nose was obviously swollen and discolored, with bits of dried blood still clinging in the corners of my nostrils. There really wasn't much that make-up could help so I didn't bother.

We drove to Cathy's house but no one answered the door. It was after ten in the morning so likely both she and Markus were at work. Noting no cars in the driveway, we circled around to the back of the yard and peered in through a glass patio door that looked directly into the living room. We could see her asleep on the couch. We banged on the back door repeatedly but she didn't budge.

"Let's go," I said. "If she's dead, I don't want to be the one to call it in!" To my surprise, Matt agreed and we headed quickly back to the front of the house. Just as we were walking up the driveway toward the street where the car was parked, Markus pulled up.

He got out of his car and scowled at us. "What are you doing on my properly?" he snarled before his mood abruptly changed. "What happened to you?" he exclaimed when he caught sight of my face.

"Your wife may have done this to me," I replied boldly.

Next to me I could hear Matt groan.

"My wife?" he barked. "Not likely. She's passed out right now from very strong pills for migraine."

"What about last night?" I countered.

"What's this all about? We spoke to the cops already. Who are you?"

"I'm a private investigator, and this is the lady who was smacked around by someone who we have reason to believe might have been your wife," Matt replied, now attempting to take control of the conversation.

"I'm the owner of the Whine and Cheese," I piped up. "You've been at my bistro. You even offered to give me a ride on your ski-do," I reminded him.

Suddenly he grinned. "I remember. But you sure looked better that night." He snickered and scratched his beard. "Cathy already had the migraine last night. She's had it for days, actually. There's no way she could have done this. I fell asleep early, but she was in no shape to drive to your place. Sorry this happened to you, though," he said. "Did you change your mind about the ski-do ride?"

"Maybe when I heal," I said, an idea suddenly springing to life in my head.

"Let me know when you do. Sorry folks, but I need to bring my wife her prescription refill, and then I have to head back to work." He nodded politely enough but it was clear that we were dismissed. He gave me one last look before heading inside.

We drove back to the bistro in silence. "That was a waste of time," I finally said.

"Not really. If what he said was true, then we know it wasn't her last night. Or if he's lying, then we know that they're in on it together."

"So in other words, we're no further ahead than we were this morning," I grumbled.

"Except that we both know that you're up to something with that exchange about going ski-doing. I don't like it, whatever it is, but I hope this time you'll keep me in the loop so I can keep an eye on you and try to talk some sense into you," he said with an air of resignation. "Are you up for a little hike?" His abrupt change in topic took me by surprise.

"I'm not really in the best shape for exercise right now," I groaned.

"Not exercise, Mali. I thought we'd just look for Billy on the trails, but only if you're up for it. I'd like to hear about what he saw last night and thank him for saving you." He gave my hand a protective little squeeze.

"I can definitely do that. I'd like to thank him too. Let me get some sandwiches ready for him."

Matt helped and we took off in search of Billy. We didn't have to go far, and I was relieved since my thigh had started to throb. Seeing Matt, Billy was about to bolt until Matt held up the food bag. "We made you some sandwiches, Billy," he said loudly. "And we just wanted to thank you. My name is Matt. We've met before."

He approached cautiously, constantly scanning the area. He reached out his hand tentatively, and Matt handed him the bag.

"Thanks for saving Amalia last night. We both appreciate it and just wanted to ask you what you saw. It might help us find who did it."

Billy looked at him suspiciously, then looked inside the bag.

"Go ahead and eat, Billy. We can talk later," I suggested. "Maybe you'll be more comfortable coming to see me when you're ready. We only need a few minutes of your time."

He shook his head. "I didn't see much. Saw that woman talking to you and the pig in the afternoon and then at night I heard the yelling and saw this other woman attacking you. I heard her voice. It wasn't the same as the woman from earlier in the day. Then she ran to the street and not long after I heard a car."

"How did you get Amalia inside?" Matt asked.

"I carried her, put her on the couch. Nice place, I wouldn't mind sleeping there. I ran a cloth under hot water, put it on your leg where the icicle was and it melted enough so I could pull it out without causing more damage. It wasn't in very deep. Then I wrapped more clothes, dish towels, I think, around your leg as tight as I could. Sorry if they're ruined."

"Why did you leave?" Matt asked.

"Because I knew they'd come," he said simply.

"Who?" I asked.

"The people who are after me. I can hear their voices right now, but they're far away. When they get closer, I have hide."

"Billy, when you take your medicine, do you still hear the voices?" I asked gently.

He looked pensive and took his time answering. "Yes," he finally said, "but they're not as loud. They're further away. Sometimes very far away, and then they don't bother me too much."

"Do you want to take medicine again and make it better?"

"Don't know," he said, then kept repeating it softly, scanning the area.

"What's your last name, Billy?" Matt asked gently. I thought he didn't hear, but to my surprise, after a few moments he answered, "Rockport."

"Do you want us to contact your family? Do you have family?" I asked.

"Don't know," he said again. "I better go. Thanks for the food." He hurried away and stopped once to wave then sprinted off the path.

Matt and I made our way back to the bistro where I took some Tylenol and then set to work in the kitchen despite Matt's protest. "I've got work to do, Matt. I won't serve the customers tonight, but I have to cook. Your company might be able to run itself, but I don't have that luxury. You're more than welcome to help, if you like.

Here, chop these apples. We're making Bavarian Apple Torte and Easy Cheesy Enchiladas tonight."

"Am I getting paid for this?" he joked.

I winked then said suggestively, "I'll find a way to pay you."

He laughed heartily. "I won't turn you down, but the winking and sexy look isn't quite working with that swollen face of yours," he said and kissed me gently on the tip of my nose.

"Now, how about you tell me what evil plan you have cooking in that head of yours since you're thinking about ski-doing with Markus?"

We set to work and I laid out my thoughts. To my surprise, he didn't tell me not to get involved. Maybe he was finally realizing that it was pointless. Before we knew it, we'd exchanged some ideas and finished all the cooking.

And by Sunday night, I was ready to face the public again and hoped that Markus would be coming by with his ski-do gang. I was anxious to put our plan into motion.

BAVARIAN APPLE TORTE

This is like a super easy cheesecake on top of a homemade flaky crust and topped with apples.

Crust:
- ½ cup margarine (or butter, doesn't matter)
- ⅓ cup granulated white sugar
- 1 cup flour
- Or you can use a store bought pie crust

Cheesecake:
- 1 softened brick of cream cheese, any kind (I use light, of course)
- 1 teaspoon vanilla
- ¼ cup granulated white sugar
- 1 egg
- 1 teaspoon of lemon juice

Topping:
- 5 or 6 apples (I prefer Granny Smith, but any kind is fine)

- 1 teaspoon ground cinnamon
- 1 tablespoon white granulated sugar
- Optional: handful of raisons or white chocolate chips

Crust: combine margarine and sugar until smooth. Add flour and mix well. I usually just use my hands when I'm mixing in the flour. Spread mixture onto bottom of a round pan or baking dish that is sprayed lightly with cooking spray. I usually use an eight or nine inch round glass baking dish and just press the dough around as evenly as possible. If you can, you can press the dough slightly up the side of the pan a little but it's not necessary.

Set aside for now.

Make the cheesecake filling- mix all the ingredients until well combined and then spread over crust.

Topping: peel and dice or slice the apples, mix with cinnamon and the sugar, toss well, and then pour over top of the filling.

Bake at 400 Fahrenheit for ten minutes then reduce temperature to 350 Fahrenheit for about 25 minutes. Remove and cool in the pan that it's in. Once it's cooled, you can slice it in the pan or dish that it's in. There's no need to try to remove it and transfer it elsewhere. It's good warm or cold. I haven't decided which way I like it better yet.

CHAPTER TWENTY-TWO

Sunday night was busy. The previous nights I had stayed in the kitchen but my leg was already healing and my face was a bit less puffy so it was time to brave the crowd. Nora had been racked by guilt when she'd found out what had happened, blaming herself for not having come home that night and going to Leonardo's instead. She was debating about getting back together with him.

Chloé had been equally shocked, which helped ease her anger at me. She hadn't said anything, but I knew she was still miffed that I had questioned her new beau, despite having defended me to him. I wondered if he'd mentioned the note to her but I didn't dare ask.

I felt the hackles on my neck rise at the same time that I sensed the door opening. Turning quickly, I groaned in frustration. The Aliens. As I approached my parents, I could see their smiles freeze, then droop, then completely turn upside down as I got closer.

"*Bazd meg*, Amalia, *mi történt?*" What happened, my father barked at me, making some customers jump at the sound of his voice.

"Come sit down and I'll tell you," I said wearily and

185

shushed them as I led them to a corner near the piano area. I filled them in with as few details as possible but there really was no way to downplay any of it. They insisted that I sleep at their place until I assured them that Nora was still with me. Nicole would be returning to her own place as she hadn't heard from Sean and everything seemed to have returned to normal in her life.

I also mentioned that Matt was making sure the bistro was being watched whenever he himself wasn't around. Just when I thought I had the situation under control, and that they were about to leave, my dad invited himself to sleep on my couch for a couple of nights. "You can't, Dad. Matt's been sleeping on the couch!" I whined as my aneurism twitched.

His eyebrows shot up in surprise. "He's not sleeping with *you*?" I blushed furiously. Naturally, I hadn't mentioned the rest of my injuries, deciding that they didn't need to know about my stabbed leg and injured elbow, and that Matt was afraid to jostle me in his sleep, hence the couch.

"He's been standing guard from the living room." I left it at that.

"Well, he can go home tonight, because I will sleep on the couch," he replied, as though he was doing us a favor. I groaned but there was no talking him out of it. He was determined to protect his little girl. What he thought he could do, at his age, and with a bad leg, was beyond me. I would feel safer if it was my mother.

They had actually come to the bistro for a rare night out so I brought them a glass of Ball Buster, a nice Shiraz based wine and some pâté and crackers, smiling sweetly as I placed a glass in front of my dad. It was my way of having the last word, though I certainly hadn't won the round. My only hope was that he wouldn't sleep in his underwear.

I had a sudden flashback to my childhood of him lounging on the couch in his white underwear and matching undershirt and of me begging him to put clothes on since Nicole, who was thirteen at the time, was coming over. His stance had been that it was his house therefore he had a right to be comfortable. I explained that this was Canada and young girls were not supposed to see their friend's fathers in their skivvies. Here he could be arrested for something like that. I shuddered at the memory and shook myself back to reality.

I made the rounds through the crowd and smiled politely at everyone's shocked reaction to my face. I had decided to make the best of it and hammed things up by wearing one of the bistro t-shirts that said in bold red "Life's a Bitch, have a glass." Bitch being a wine, of course. To keep things interesting for myself, I gave everyone who asked about my face a different answer, each time something far-fetched. I ran into a tree. The tree won. Drank too much wine, couldn't remember. Cat fight. And my favorite: This was what I look like when I donn't wear make-up.

I saw movement and looked up to see my parents waving. My dad would take mum home and then return at closing time. I joined them and walked them to the door. As they walked out, Markus and his gang walked in. I gave Jeff a big smile and some of the tension eased from his face. He smiled back, albeit tightly, then his eyes widened at the sight of my face, though he made no comment.

They gathered around the bar while Chloé, Nora and I re-arranged some of the smaller tables and chairs to accommodate the group. They hadn't made reservations this time but we managed to get them set up near the piano in the section that my parents had just vacated. I beckoned to Markus to indicate that their space was ready and he grinned as he passed me.

"You're looking better today, sweetheart. Are you feeling up for that ride with me yet?" I looked him straight in the eyes and asked "What about your wife? Won't she mind?"

"She won't know. Guys don't rat each other out like that. She hates ski-doing anyway. She comes along a couple of times a year just to keep me from nagging her, but that's about it."

"All right," I said, "But how about a quick spin tonight to see how I like it? Plus, I'm still pretty sore from the attack." His eyes lit up.

"It's a date." Ugh! What was I thinking, and why had Matt agreed to this?

We served their table quickly and then I dashed upstairs to where Matt was napping on the couch. "The plan is on schedule; it's show time," I whispered in his ear and then gave it a gentle nibble until he stirred. "Markus is here. He's taking me for a little spin tonight." Matt was fully awake now and was expecting this after I'd spent hours talking him into it.

"I still don't like it, but if you call me before you get on, and keep your cell phone on, I'll be able to keep tabs on you. I'll have it on speakerphone and have Nora record it all with her own phone, just in case. Just keep dropping little hints along the way so that we know where you are at all times, okay? And try to get him to stop for a while; that's when you can try to get information about his wife and Nancy. It's got to be one of those two."

I nodded then gave him the bad news. "I'll stick to the plan, but there's a little hitch. My dad insisted on sleeping here tonight so he'll be here too. You'll have to explain this all to him somehow."

He swore. "That's the last thing we need! Damn it. Okay, I'll figure out a way to deal with him. Don't worry about a thing here." He kissed me tenderly.

"How come you're agreeing to all this considering that previously you lectured me to stay out of it?" I couldn't help but ask.

"Trust me, if I thought he was dangerous, I wouldn't have agreed. There's still a chance, but as long as you stick to the plan, everything should be okay. I'll have Ricky out there on a ski-do too, and a couple of guys hiding in the trees, so you're not out there alone. Wherever you are, someone will be close by. And as you leave, make sure everyone around knows you're going ski-doing with him. This way, he'll know there are witnesses that saw you leave with him."

I nodded and he gently kissed my temple. "Just stick to the plan, okay? Don't deviate. Please." I nodded my consent. I had no intentions of deviating.

I went back down to the bistro, counting the minutes until I saw Markus's glass almost empty. I had filled Nora, Chloé and Nicole in on the plan as briefly as possible, and Nora knew to head upstairs as soon as Markus and I headed toward the front door. I moved to his table to get the plan in motion. "Are we ready for that ride?" I said boisterously in front of his gang. He licked his lips hungrily and my skin crawled.

"Sure, let's go. I never keep a lady waiting. Boys, don't wait up for me," he grinned at his friends as he stood. Those in the gang looked at me curiously.

"I'll meet you at the door in a moment; I have to get my coat and boots," I said, and rushed back to my office where I'd hung my coat earlier. I joined him a few moments later. "All set, let's go!" As I followed him out, I hit Matt's number on speed dial and then shoved the phone into my bra and left my coat zipper slightly pulled down.

Markus pulled on his helmet and then climbed onboard, instructing me to get on behind him. "No helmet for me?" I asked, slightly concerned.

"Sorry, but I didn't know I'd have company today. Don't worry, I'll be careful. We'll just travel these trails and I'll go slowly."

I climbed onboard and sat behind him. "Okay, I'm all set to go into the trails," I called out from behind him.

"Put your arms around me," he ordered, and I grimaced behind him but obeyed since I had no choice.

He started the ski-do and we moved forward, slowly. We headed onto the trail and he kept his word, driving at a slow pace. He must have felt me relax behind him, and in response went just a little faster so that I'd clutch him more tightly.

"Everything is so pretty out here at night! I have a friend who camps out around here sometimes; maybe we'll see him," I yelled out for him to hear, letting him know that we might not be alone and also giving Matt a reference point as to where we were. Markus gave me a thumbs-up sign.

We continued onward for a few minutes before I hit his arm a couple of times and shouted, "Stop! Stop!!" He came to a halt and I hopped off, grabbing my calf and falling to the ground. "Sorry, I have a cramp; it's a bad one." I was faking, of course, but he fell for it and grabbed my calf, massaging rigorously. I let him do that for about a minute before I smiled. "Thank you so much; that's much better. Come sit next to me for a few minutes, will you? I want to make sure it doesn't come back before I get back on the ski-do." He did as I suggested and sat next to me, his shoulder brushing mine. We sat in silence for a few moments. "What's the scoop with your wife? Are you guys having problems, or do you have an open relationship?"

He looked uncomfortable suddenly, his swagger gone now that we were surrounded by trees, snow and silence. He shrugged. "She's been acting strange lately. We've been together a long time, seven years. Maybe it's that seven-year itch thing, I don't know."

"It happens. I was with someone for six years before I finally left him," I sympathized and shared some small comments about my ex, Hans. "I heard her in the grocery store one day, talking about Alphie spitting on your pizza. How long ago was that?"

"He was working at Leonardo's then and got every order wrong before I finally said something. I think he did it on purpose, too. I owed him money, and he kept

190

holding that over my head."

"Oh, did you have a loan from him too?" I asked innocently.

"Something like that," he muttered. I could sense a shift in his mood so I changed the subject.

"If Cathy finds out I am with you, will she get upset? I don't know who came after me the other night, but it's sure made me nervous. I'm not saying it was her, don't get me wrong. I believe you when you say she was passed out from her migraine pills. I just don't want to cause any trouble."

"You know; I keep thinking about that. She's not like that. She might have a crazy Irish streak in her, but I've never seen her go after anyone. She's all bark and no bite, you know? And she really did have a migraine that night. She was even throwing up. The next day, too."

"Was she friends with Valerie, Alphie's wife?" I asked casually. He laughed.

"Uh, no. I can't say they were buddies."

"Did they even know each other?" I asked next.

He nodded. "Yeah, they met a few times through her sister. Her sister is friends with Val. I don't think either of them cared for each other, though. Val said..." he broke off, realizing his mistake and I pounced on it.

"Valerie said what? You sound like you were friends with her? She seems nice. I met her a couple of times." I was lying about her seeming nice, of course, but I was trying to soften my question.

"Yeah, Val and I know each other. We may have had some history. I never told Cathy, but maybe she heard something. Maybe Val mentioned something to Nancy, and then Nancy told Cathy. You know how women talk." He laughed nervously.

"Nancy? From the post office?" I asked, the surprise clear in my voice.

"Yeah, she's Cathy's sister. You know her, too?" he asked in return.

191

"I've met her a few times. I didn't realize they were sisters. It seems like everyone around here knows each other or is related," I tried to joke and to change the subject. "How about we head back now, Markus? Thanks for bringing me out here; it's been fun. You seem like a sweet guy. I hope things work out for you and Cathy."

He shrugged. "Yeah, she's okay, I guess. We've just been through a lot lately. I guess I can be a jerk sometimes. Come on then, let's go." He hopped to his feet with an agility that surprised me considering his girth and held his hand out to me to help me up. I stood and gave my calf a quick rub and pretended to walk out the cramp.

"Hey, before I forget. What do you know about Jeff, the guy that my friend Chloé is dating? I'm not so sure about him. I don't get a good vibe." For some reason, I suddenly felt like Markus was one of my pals. He really wasn't that bad once he dropped the macho act.

He scratched his beard, choosing his words carefully. "I wouldn't trust him. He was always defending Alphie. It seems to me that they were kind of tight, you know? I know they sometimes hung out together, though Jeff would never admit it because he knows that no one in the crowd liked him. I never saw him with any women though, so I can't say what he's like with them." He shrugged but didn't offer any more.

"Thanks for being honest, Markus. I'll keep my guard up around him. All right, I'm ready. I think I'll be okay," I said and got onboard behind him.

We headed back towards the house and about halfway there I could hear the sounds of another snow mobile in the distance. I became nervous, thinking Ricky would blow his cover.

"Is it my imagination, or do I hear another snow mobile?" I shouted out to Markus. He eased back on the throttle and went even slower and the whine of another sled could be heard. It seemed to be approaching fast but I couldn't tell from which direction. Markus shrugged and picked up speed.

We were just rounding a bend when we saw the other ski-do. Its headlight beamed on us and Markus moved as far to the right as he could on the trail. It zoomed past us and I could see Markus's shoulders relax slightly. Not more than a minute passed though, when we heard it again, this time bearing down on us from behind.

"Oh, my God, he's coming right at us!" I screeched, having turned my head for a look and seeing the headlight far too close for comfort. A moment later, it veered right into us. I lost my grip on Markus and tried to get a firmer grip on the ski-do with my legs, but then it hit us again and I went flailing off, landing hard on my already injured elbow.

Markus quickly pulled over and came running toward me, but the other ski-do had turned and was doubling back at us again. "It's coming straight at us again!" I screamed to Markus, who jumped off the trail and into a tight cluster of trees just in time. The ski-do was now headed straight at me. I screamed at the top of my lungs and tried to roll out of the way, only to see the headlights bearing down on me as my head struck a big rock at the side of the trail.

Through the searing pain, I saw something hurtle past me at the last second and lunge at the driver, sending the ski-do off course and the driver tumbling. I could hear grappling and shouting as I fought to hold consciousness. I could hear Matt yelling at me from my bra but I couldn't make my arms move; then I could hear my dad's voice yelling in a panic, also from inside my bra.

And then the darkness won the battle.

CHAPTER TWENTY-THREE

Through the fog I could hear shouting. It would fade in and out, grow louder, then softer. I tried to open my eyes but it was exhausting, tried to move an arm, excruciating. I concentrated hard and was able to wiggle a leg. I remember thinking, "I'm not paralyzed, maybe I'll try again after a nap," and then I faded away again.

More shouting and then something that smelled awful—ammonia and eucalyptus. There was a stinging feeling and then a *whoosh* as my brain jumped into action. My eyes shot open and I yelled, remembering the ski-do and Matt and my dad shouting and the headlight bearing down on me. As I was yelling, Ricky and Markus's features came into focus and I peed a little. I took a deep breath and panted a few times as my heartbeat fought to find an even tempo.

"Can you move?" Ricky asked, his big fish eyes looking down at me.

"I don't know. I think so," I answered, then started to flail my limbs. When I moved my left arm, I cried out in pain and remembered that I'd smashed my already injured elbow again.

"Left elbow...doesn't feel good. Head hurts. Otherwise peachy." I attempted a smile and then heard my dad's voice from my bra again. "Amalia, *bazd meg*, Amalia, hallo?"

"'Excuse me," I said, reaching into my bra with my good hand. "I'm okay, Dad. I'll see you soon. Is Matt there?" I was greeted with more swearing but somewhere in between, he mentioned that Matt was already on his way to me. "Okay, you're going back into my pocket, Dad, so you can still hear everything, but I have to go now. I'll see you soon." I didn't want to hang up, just in case something went wrong.

Markus looked ashen. "Hey! We lived," I said.

He nodded. "I should have insisted that you wear my helmet. I'm sorry. I never thought...we were just talking about him...I don't know why..." He kept interrupting himself, and I looked at Ricky questioningly.

"Let me help you up, Amalia," he said and took my good arm gently, bringing me up to a sitting position. "There, just sit. Now look over there." He pointed and I followed his finger to some lumps in the snow just a few feet away. As I looked, Ricky directed the flashlight he was holding and Billy came into focus and waved. I could make out what seemed like blood on his face and as I looked closer I could see that he had a firm grip on Jeff. From time to time he'd thrash about like an angry crocodile, and then I noticed that he appeared to be hog-tied. For some crazy reason, it made me think of Chicha, and I wondered if she'd been fed.

"Can I lie down until Matt gets here?" I asked politely.

Markus sat next to me and pulled me gently toward him so that I was leaning on him. "It's really best if you stay alert, Amalia. Just lean against me so you don't have to use any of your strength. Help should be here any moment." I nodded and let myself lean against him.

We soon heard the sound of ski-dos approaching and Ricky waved his flashlight. Matt pulled up a few feet away from us and then two other snow mobiles arrived. Officer Sean and his partner approached Billy and Jeff while Matt rushed to me. He knelt next to me in the snow. "Are you okay? I'll never forgive myself for letting you go. You're bleeding." He touched some blood that appeared to trickle from my temple. "I really do have to wrap you in bubble wrap, don't I," he said yet again.

"It wasn't your choice to "let" me go or not," I bristled, albeit weakly. He knew damn well how I reacted when someone tried to tell me what to do.

"It's okay. You need to relax now. You can get mad at me later." He grinned then gave me a gentle kiss. Then to Markus and Ricky, "Can you guys help me get her onto the ski-do?"

They loaded me onboard behind him and this time Markus placed his enormous helmet over my head. "It's better than nothing," he mumbled apologetically as the weight of it pushed down on my sore cranium.

"Are you able to grab onto me until we get home? It's only a couple of minutes away," Matt said. I grabbed onto him as hard as I could and we moved forward slowly. When we got back, there was an ambulance waiting, and despite my protests, I was lifted inside just as my dad came running out dressed in pajamas that were inside-out. He spoke with the ambulance driver to find out where they were taking me, then climbed inside for a moment to let me know he'd get my mom and then see me there.

Matt rode in the back with me, never letting go of my hand. Exhausted by everything, I let myself drift off while enjoying the warmth of his hand holding mine. Just before drifting off, I peeked out from below my eyelashes in time to see him take a swipe at his cheeks with the back of his other hand.

I was admitted to the hospital just for the night, and I was ready to leave by noon the next day. My dad had picked up my mom before coming to the hospital in the middle of the night and now both of them, along with

Matt, were looking at me gravely.

The doctor came to give instructions and looked at me more closely. "Ah. Ms. Kis! Yes, I remember you. You have a bit of a concussion...again...as well as a broken elbow this time. You already know what to do about the concussion, yes?" He waited for me to nod before he looked at Matt. "Be sure that she takes it easy. Lots of sleep, Tylenol as needed. She will need help in the bath— do not get her splint wet. And no physical activity." Matt took the hint: no hanky-panky. We'd been through this speech before.

My parents met us back at my home where Nicole, Nora and Chloé were all waiting for me. I noticed a bunch of bags by the front door.

"Whose bags are these?" I asked, my eyes immediately landing on my mother.

"I don't know," she replied, looking at Matt curiously. He shook his head and shrugged.

Nora piped up from the living room. "It's my stuff, Mali. I've decided to go back to Craig. I think I've had enough excitement for a while. I'm ready to go back. I think Chicha misses the other animals, anyway. Thank you for everything, but I'll get going now so that you can relax with your family. You can fill me in on Thursday night." She gave me a cautious hug, gently removed Hummer who was lying on top of one bag, scooped up all her belongings and left. Although I should have been happy, part of me felt as though my only child had just moved out. Crazy, of course, since she was so much older than me.

"We're going too," Nicole said. "We just wanted to make sure you are okay."

"Wait! Chloé, are you okay? I don't know many details yet, but this all has to do with Jeff, doesn't it?"

She nodded. "You were right about him. I'll let Matt fill you in, but don't worry about me." She gave me a bright smile, but I could see the sadness just beyond her brave façade.

"I need a favor before you both leave. Can you take me and my mom's spot at the pole-dancing class tomorrow night? I'm not allowed to go."

My mother laid a meaty hand on my shoulder. "I going," she announced. I almost fell off the couch.

My dad was grinning from ear to ear. "Shure, Mama going. She having fun."

Nicole grinned. "I'll go with you, Mr. Kis," she volunteered, "Even though I dance for a living, I've never learned pole dancing. I'm sure it'll be fun, and you and I will have a great time. I'll pick you up before the class and I'll bring you one of our new t-shirts, if you like. We just had some new ones made that say, "Try my Forbidden Fruit." Hey, maybe you can help us this week with the cooking since Amalia needs to recover?" she gushed.

I was about to open my mouth to object when Matt thrust a glass of wine in front of my nose and commanded me to drink. He didn't normally like it when I mixed wine with Tylenol but I wasn't about to argue. I sat back to let everyone discuss my bistro and, tuning them out, started daydreaming of my mother's fried pork schnitzel. Perhaps it wouldn't be such a bad idea to let her cook in the bistro again. Maybe I should even offer her a permanent spot, one day a week.

Not soon enough, everyone left after a flurry of hugs and kisses, finally leaving me and Matt alone. I pinned him with my eyes. "One more glass, please, then fill me in, would you?"

His brows rose in surprise as he advanced toward me. "It'll be my pleasure," he grinned.

I threw a couch cushion at him. "You know what I mean. I'm dying to know how all the puzzle pieces fit together."

He brought the wine bottle and made a show of pouring me a glassful, giving me time to read the label, *Murder on my Mind.* "Oh, that's a new one! That's not from my stock, but I love it!" I exclaimed.

"I saw it the other day and thought of you. What can I say? I'm a romantic."

"You know me too well..." I grinned then got down to business. "Okay, let's hear it."

CHAPTER TWENTY-FOUR

Matt paced as he spoke, reminding me of a lawyer presenting his final summation.

"Jeff and Alphie were an odd pair. They had a love-hate thing going for each other. They'd been acquaintances for quite a while, and although they didn't particularly like each other, they both recognized themselves in each other." He took a sip of wine while he let me absorb what he'd said, then continued, back-tracking so that I could see how all the various people tied into the crime. He recapped how Valerie and Alphie were married, that Nancy and her ex, Bob, had divorced, and that Cathy and Markus were still married and hoping to work things out. None of this was really new information, and I waved my hands impatiently for him to speed up.

Sadly, I had been right when I'd once stated that everyone seemed to be connected by body parts. Valerie had slept with Bob and Markus. Alphie had slept with Cathy, and then dumped her soon after for her sister, Nancy, who slept with Alphie even though she and Val were friends. Believe it or not, though, she hadn't known that her sister Cathy had already slept with him. Nancy

201

then partnered with Jeff, but hadn't yet ended things with Alphie.

My eyes must have glazed over because he strode across the room, got a sheet of paper and a pen and wrote out their names and drew arrows connecting the names to each other, much as I'd once done. I'm a very visual person, so this helped me to connect the dots, and when I saw Nancy's name paired with Jeff, it all began to make sense.

"The night that Nancy and Alphie went to your bistro was for show. Nancy wanted people to think she was still with Alphie, even though they were supposedly trying to keep the relationship quiet. That part just never made sense, her wanting to go out in public to celebrate their supposed anniversary when it was all supposed to be hush-hush. The reality was that she and Jeff just didn't want anyone tying them together until she finalized some intricate matters with Alphie. She was sleeping with both of them at that point. Jeff was at your bistro that night, as you know, and Valerie showed up with Bob, Nancy's ex."

He took another sip of wine. "Alphie had been blackmailing Markus. He knew that he'd slept with Valerie and that Markus didn't want his wife to find out. What's even sicker, though, is that after Alphie dumped Cathy for her sister, he started blackmailing her, too, because she didn't want Markus to find out that she'd slept with him. He thought he was brilliant, blackmailing both husband and wife and couldn't help but brag to Jeff, who really was the only person who came close to being any kind of buddy to him."

Matt outlined the rest of story and all the puzzle pieces fit into place one after the other. Enter Nancy: once she and Jeff started getting more serious, he wanted her to break it off with Alphie and she said that she tried but he claimed he wasn't ready for it to end. According to him, it was over when he said it was over. Luckily, she never told Alphie that she'd hooked up with Jeff. She had only said she was tired of being the other woman.

He told her he'd taped some of their intimate moments together and threatened to show the ski-do gang if she broke up with him before he was ready to call it quits. She'd been complaining to her sister about her predicament when Cathy confided that she had slept with him too, and that he was blackmailing her as well.

I poured us both some more wine and Matt fixed us a late lunch. I sighed, "I shouldn't be drinking," and pushed my glass away. I was a little surprised that after two glasses of wine my head was swooning.

"Nicole made these for us. It looks like that Enchilada dish I helped you make the other day but with a different kind of cheese on top. I'll cut it up for you so you don't have to struggle with it." He helped me to the table and stood behind me to cut my food, resting his cheek gently against mine. He took the seat next to mine just in case I needed help, and then resumed the story.

"After Nancy found out about her sister being blackmailed, she told Jeff, who'd already heard about it, but he hadn't known that the target was her sister. When he heard about the supposed sex tapes, he was raging mad. Together, they concocted a little plan."

Engrossed in the story, he absentmindedly fed me some food off his plate. I shrugged and chewed. I had already finished what was on my plate and was hungry for more.

"The night that Alphie was murdered, Nancy had told him to bring the tapes and suggested that they could watch them together at her place after dinner. The plan was that Jeff would jump him, rough him up a bit, get the tapes and destroy them, and then Nancy could finally dump Alphie, leaving her and Jeff to live happily ever after.

"You know part of what happened next. Things didn't quite go according to the plan. Val and Bob showed up and saw Alphie and Nancy, plus Val also saw Markus, who she'd slept with recently, so they left right away. She hadn't known that this was the ski-do gang's new hangout. Alphie rushed out after them, so Nancy went after him to see what would happen. By the time they got outside, Valerie and Bob were already driving away. Alphie started to head for Nancy's car, but as luck would have it, Jeff had just gone out for a smoke and was over by his ski-do, which was parked near your garage."

I grumbled a bit at that part. That was my personal space and visitors were supposed to stay in the parking lot area dedicated to the bistro.

"Other than Nancy, no one else was around, so Jeff took advantage of the situation. He called Alphie over to where he was standing and then demanded the video tape, proudly telling him that he and Nancy were dating. Alphie laughed at him and then admitted that there was no tape, and that he'd just been toying with her. Then he started to insult both of them and said nasty things about Nancy in particular. Jeff told him to knock it off, and then they started shoving each other around and the violence quickly escalated."

"Alphie then pulled his hunting knife out and started slashing at Jeff. This is the same knife that was later found in your bistro, the night Nancy tried to attack you. I'll get to that later, though. But Jeff hadn't counted on any weapons, figuring they'd just get into a fist fight at some point. Alphie had him backed up against your garage, trying to slash him and managed to gouge his wrist. Nancy rushed at him, trying to intervene, which is how she got the gash on her hand. Jeff then took advantage of the distraction, reached up, and grabbed an icicle. Supposedly, he'd never meant to kill him, and in fact it hadn't even crossed his mind, but somehow Alphie lost his footing and fell, eyeball first, onto the icicle.

"They panicked at the sudden turn of events and had to act fast before anyone else showed up, so they dragged him into your garage, removed his coat, since Nancy was afraid that some of her or Jeff's blood may have splattered onto it when he sliced them, stuffed him underneath your patio table and then Nancy drove home. She and Alphie had taken her car, so that made her get-away simple. Jeff went inside the bistro to join his pals, as though nothing had happened. He'd taken a quick trip to the restroom to tidy his wound and then mentioned to his buddies that he'd slipped on a patch of ice and fell on his way inside. This was the perfect crime, of course, since the icicle eventually melted from Alphie's body heat and because it was warm in your garage."

"This is all so tragic. So much greed and... unfaithfulness," I said sadly. "Why did Valerie slash my tire? And why did Nancy come after me?" There were still loose ends.

"Valerie just wanted you to stop digging around. She was happy he was dead. This way, she would eventually collect his life insurance and they also had mortgage insurance on the house, so the house would be paid off too. She'd known about his infidelities for years but didn't care because she was just as unfaithful. Everyone just assumed she was sweet and innocent. She was also nervous that the killer may have been Markus and that she still had a soft spot for him, so if it was him, she didn't want him to be caught. I guess she didn't stop to think that if she was still a suspect in his murder, she couldn't collect the insurance money."

He went on to tell me that Nancy was the other one to slash my tire, using Alphie's hunting knife. She just didn't like how I kept questioning her and figured I knew something and was hoping to scare me off.

"When that didn't work, and after that note that you left, she was sure you were on to her and Jeff and figured she had to get rid of you. The cops didn't make her nervous, since Officer Sean really dropped the ball on this one, being as pre-occupied as he was, but you did. She was going to use the knife on you, but had dropped it when she ran after you. She'd been startled when you bolted outside rather than continuing into the kitchen area."

To my relief, Matt told me that the driver in my parking lot looking for directions was just pure luck for her, but she would have found a way to get in eventually, even if she had had to break a window. She didn't realize that I had friends staying with me, and thought I lived alone.

"Billy!" I suddenly remembered. "Billy had saved me that night from Nancy, but he also saved me from Jeff. I remembered seeing that he was bleeding. Is he okay?"

Matt smiled. "He's better than okay. He was quite lucid that night and understood that he had to go to the hospital to get his wound treated. He'd seen Ricky helping you, so he figured he could trust him if you did. Ricky drove him to the hospital and already knew about Billy and his medical condition since I'd mentioned it to him a few times. The doctors were able to convince Billy to resume taking his medication and after only a day, you can see a difference. Remember when he finally told us his last name? We were able to track down his parents since there's only one Rockport listed in the Robin phone book, so we got a lucky break there."

He gave me a gentle hug. "I made sure that Ricky gave him your number so he could keep in touch, and I told him to let Billy know we'll visit in a couple of days. They're going to keep him in the hospital for a while until he's mentally stable, maybe even for a couple of weeks. The parents were so happy that he was found. They'd been arguing about something and Billy misunderstood, thinking it was about him and that they'd be better off without him, which is why he'd left. Of course, he hadn't known where to go. He had happy memories of hiking on those trails with his folks, so he ended up making that his home."

"I want to go to see him tomorrow," I insisted.

He looked like he was about to argue then thought better of it. "Fine, but have a nice long sleep first." I conceded. After all, I love lazy mornings, and if he would be there with me, it would be even better.

"How about Officer Sean? Has he been behaving? When you came to the rescue, I noticed that he was there too?"

"Yes, he's been staying away from Nicole. He wouldn't look me in the eye yesterday, but he did his job. That's all I can ask."

We sat in silence for a moment while I digested all the information. "Hey, why didn't my parents stick around to hear all this? It's not like them to just leave like that."

"I filled them in earlier. An abbreviated version, of course, since I knew that's what you'd prefer. When I said I'd stay here with you, they were relieved. I'm not sure, but your father may have offered to pay me. Maybe something was lost in the translation, though!" He snickered to himself as I rolled my eyes.

The more I thought about it, the more I knew that that would be just like my dad. He'd probably offer him a dowry to take me off his hands! No doubt there'd be extra if Matt could convince me to take an accounting class.

"Wait. There's still loose ends. The third bunch of flowers that Alphie bought, who were they for? And what about Bob? The guy we never had a chance to track down. Nancy's ex." Loose ends were pet peeve of mine.

"I wondered the same thing and snooped around a bit more so that you could officially retire as a sleuth. But I couldn't find out who the flowers were for. They could have been for his mom, for all we know. As for Bob, he knew Val from when he'd been married to Nancy since they were friends. He and Valerie had only recently starting seeing each other and were going out for drinks that night. There was nothing serious going on between them other than a fling. Oh, and by the way, the car that was following Markus the same night that I was? It was Cathy. She knew he'd cheated on her and was suspicious that it was still going on. She'd found out from Nancy, since Val had confided in her. You know, I think Markus and Cathy are going to survive this. They both still love each other and I think they'll work it out."

"Yes, I think so too. What about Chloé? Was she ever in any danger?" I asked, feeling guilty for having encouraged her to see Jeff to see if she could find out anything.

"No, remember, Jeff never actually meant to kill Alphie. When he hooked up with Chloé, it was because he and Nancy didn't want anyone to tie them together right after the murder, so he had to distance himself from her and dated your friend as a cover. He did seem to like her. I do have some bad news for you though," he hesitated.

"Bad news? And all this has been good news so far?" I squawked incredulously, startling Hummer who had been lounging happily on my lap. He gave me a disgusted look before slinking away.

"Well, you're really not going to like this. Remember how you and Mr. Leonardo were almost friendly with each other? Well, when Nora broke up with him for good, she kind of let it slip that she'd been living with you. So now he believes you're somehow responsible for the breakup and has gone back to hating you with renewed vigor. I just thought I'd warn you."

I groaned. "And I was so close to being able to order pizza!" I sighed in frustration and Matt grinned and reached his arm behind me, massaging my neck gently. I soon forgot all my troubles as he leaned over and whispered in my ear.

"How about a nice, hot, silky bubble bath, Ms. Kis? I must follow the doctor's orders, after all." My skin broke out in a goosebumps as I pictured it, and as Matt gently tugged at my top with his teeth.

"Oh, yes," I giggled. "That sounds like a wonderful idea." His lips hungrily met mine and we left a trail of clothing behind on our way but never actually made it into the tub until much, much later.

EASY CHEESY ENCHILADAS

Forget about rolling them, these are layered and stacked, baked and sliced. It doesn't get easier.

- 1 pound (regular size package) of ground beef (I use lean or extra lean- use what you want, but strain off the fat after cooking)
- 1 can spicy red pepper tomatoes or any kind of canned spicy diced-style tomatoes
- 3 or 4 small flour tortillas (whatever kind you like- I never tried this with a corn tortilla though, which isn't as soft in consistency)
- 2 cups of your favorite shredded cheese (mozzarella or cheddar work well)
- 1 teaspoon each chili powder and garlic powder
- Sour cream for garnish (optional)

Brown beef in skillet until cooked, drain off fat. Stir in can of tomatoes and the spices and simmer for about 5 minutes.

In a deep round pie plate or dish or some sort, place 2 tablespoons of meat mixture on bottom and spread around. Then place 1 tortilla that should just fit the dish. Add a layer of meat and a layer of cheese, then layer again with tortilla and meat and cheese.

Continue until no more meat mixture is left (usually after 2 or 3 layers of tortillas). Make sure the top layer ends with meat mixture and cheese. Bake in 350 Celsius oven until cheese is melty.

Remove from oven and allow to cool for about five minutes then slice and serve with sour cream, maybe some rice. Guacamole or sliced avocados are really nice on it too.

Now don't go thinking that Amalia actually stops snooping into things. How can she, when someone deliberately tries to entangle her in another murder in *Feta and the Fat Bastard?*